Cute Little Gifts to Crochet

25 quick and easy crocheted miniatures to make and give for special occasions

Cute Little Gifts to Crochet

25 quick and easy crocheted miniatures to make and give for special occasions

Annie Obaachan

Quantum Books

A QUANTUM BOOK

This book is produced by
Quantum Books
6 Blundell Street
London N7 9BH

ISBN: 978-1-84573-517-3

QUMHC2A

Printed and bound in China by 1010 Printing Interntional Limited

Design: Jeremy Tilston
Photographer: Simon Pask
Managing Editor: Julie Brooke
Project Editor: Samantha Warrington
Assistant Editor: Jo Morley
Production Manager: Rohana Yusof
Publisher: Sarah Bloxham

Contents

Cute, Cute, Cute

Welcome to the Wonderful World of Amigurumi

What is amigurumi?

The word *amigurumi* is a combination of the words *ami* and *nuigurumi*. *Ami* means "knit/crochet" in Japanese and *nuigurumi* means "stuffed toy". Put them together, and you have a crocheted stuffed toy.

No one really knows where amigurumi came from. There have always been handmade toys in Japan. Japan has a rich history in textiles, as we can see in weaving for kimonos, the Japanese traditional costume. But there is no such history of knitting or crochet. The Japanese simply took these Western crafts and, instead of using them for purely functional items like socks and scarves, they started to create little animals. Nowadays there are hundreds of amigurumi exhibitions and clubs, not only in Japan but all over the world.

The birth of amigurumi may have been greatly influenced by Japanese traditional doll culture, which has a long history. Hina Matsuri, a doll festival in honor of Girls' Day, is celebrated on the third of March every year, just in time for the peach blossoms. The Odairi-sama/Ohina-sama dolls, representing the Emperor and the Empress, are displayed for this festival by each family with a daughter to ensure her future happiness. This set of dolls tends to be handed down from generation to generation with love, respect, and a sense of history. Boys also have a special doll festival in May.

The dolls stay with Japanese children all their lives, lifting their spirits in times of stress and trouble. Amigurumi animals are an extension of this doll culture, brightening up cloudy days and providing a source of comfort at the toughest of times.

The last few years have witnessed a flowering of Japanese subcultures worldwide. A particularly popular feature of this phenomenon is the Japanese kawaii culture. The closest translation of *kawaii* in English is "cute". From Hello Kitty to Pokémon, anime to manga, cute Japanese characters have swarmed across the world and conquered our hearts. Amigurumi creations also swam with this kawaii-tide. Small, cute, and easy to make, how could they fail to captivate us?

In Japan, people like to keep these animals with them throughout the day. You will see them hanging off bags next to lucky charms, or sitting atop computers and piles of work in the office. Amigurumi characters can comfort and reassure us in this hectic world, secretly saying: "Why don't you take a little break and relax?"

Anyone can master amigurumi, and there are no limits to what you can create. Grab some yarn and crochet hooks, get comfortable by the fire, and start making your own little world.

Tools and Materials

Basic Crochet Kit

Crochet hooks come in a great variety of materials, from wooden and plastic to chunky steel and even ivory. All come in different shapes and sizes. Different countries have different sizing systems – which can be confusing – so always double-check your hook against the conversion charts. Check also that you are using the correct size hook as indicated in the pattern. All of the patterns in this book use a 3mm crochet hook. However, remember that experimenting with various weights and types of yarn will require different-sized hooks; the important thing is to use a hook that will give a nice tight crochet with the selected yarn.

Knitter's pins with large heads (useful for pinning shapes)

Tapestry needle for sewing up

Split stitch markers for marking the beginnings of rounds.

Tape measure

Sharp scissors

Tweezers to help with stuffing

Embroidery needle for embroidering faces and details.

Embroidery thread

Well-spun yarns are the ideal choice if you want to achieve neat, tidy work.

Fine crochet cotton (lace) thread has a firm texture that is good for very small details. Its thickness is given in numbers, i.e., 5, 10, and so on. The higher the number, the finer the thread.

4-ply yarn is good in general, especially for making smaller items.

Double knit (DK) yarn is good for making large pieces, but make sure the crochet is as tight as possible so the stuffing can't be seen. You can achieve different results in amigurumi depending on what size or type of yarn you use, even when you are working on the same pattern. The thicker the yarn, the bigger your amigurumi will be! Just remember to use the right size hook for your yarn – look on the ball band for this information.

Mohair is good for anything you want to have a fluffy texture.

Fancy yarns, such as tweed-effect wools, lurex and bouclé yarns, can be used to create texture and add interesting decorative details.

Cotton wadding is the most commonly used material for stuffing amigurumi, but you could also use scraps of yarn for the really tiny parts.

Small wooden sticks for any parts that need a bit of support to stay upright.

Reading Patterns

If this is the first time that you have used crochet patterns, you might feel like you are learning a new language. However, you will soon begin to recognize the abbreviations used in crochet. The abbreviations make patterns shorter and easier to follow.

Let's learn the new crochet language.

Crochet Abbreviations

alt	alternate
approx	approximately
beg	begin/beginning
bet	between
ch	chain stitch
cm	centimetre(s)
col	colour
cont	continue
dc	double crochet
dc2tog	double crochet 2 stitches together
dtr	double treble crochet
dec	decrease/decreases/decreasing
foll	follow/follows/following
htr	half-treble crochet
inc	increase/increases/increasing
mm	millimetre
rep	repeat(s)
sl st	slip stitch
st(s)	stitch(es)
tog	together
tr	treble
tr2tog	treble crochet 2 stitches together
yo	yarn over hook
*	repeat that step

Now, it's time to step into the hook-sizing world.

Both letters and numbers can appear on the packaging of crochet hooks. The metric sizing is the actual measurement of the hook. The letter is the U.S. sizing range. Lettering may vary, so always rely on the metric sizings.

METRIC	USA
2.5 mm	B
3 mm	C
3.25 mm	D
3.5 mm	E
4 mm	F
4.25 mm	G
5 mm	H
5.5 mm	I
6 mm	J
7 mm	K
8 mm	L
9 mm	M
10 mm	N
15 mm	P

How to read a Japanese crochet chart
On the Japanese chart, each stitch is shown as follows:

- **Magic ring:** tiny circle in the middle of circular chart ○
- **Double crochet:** cross x or +
- **Treble crochet:** T symbol Ŧ
- **Chain stitch:** tiny oval o
- **Increasing:** arrow pointing toward the centre of the diagram >
- **Decreasing:** arrow pointing away from the centre of the diagram <
- **Slip stitch:** black oval ●
- **Back loop:** straight line _

Follow the chart from the centre to the outside, then move to the non-circular part of the chart, if there is one shown above the circular part. Always follow the chart anti-clockwise.

Crochet Techniques

Crochet is all about mixing really simple techniques with more elaborate flourishes. Once you get the hang of making chains, you are ready to progress to a variety of fancy stitches.

Holding the hook and yarn

Learning how to hold the hook and yarn correctly is the first step to crochet. Most people hold the hook and yarn as they would a pencil or a knife, but you should experiment to find the most comfortable way for you.

Mastering the slipknot

Making a slipknot is the first step in any project. Master the slipknot technique, and you are on your way to super crochet!

Make a loop in the yarn. With your hook, catch the ball end of the yarn and draw it through the loop. Pull firmly on the yarn and hook to tighten the knot and create your first loop.

Making a chain

1. Before making a chain, you need to place the slipknot on a hook. To make a chain, hold the tail end of the yarn with the left hand and bring the yarn over the hook by passing the hook in front of the yarn, under, and around it.
2. Keeping the tension in the yarn taut, draw the hook and yarn through the loop.
3. Pull the yarn, hook it through the hole, and begin again, ensuring that the stitches are fairly loose. Repeat to make the number of chains required. As the chain lengthens, keep hold of the bottom edge to maintain the tension.

How to count a chain

To count the stitches, use the right side of the chain, or the side that has more visible and less twisted 'V' shapes, as shown. Do not count the original slip stitch, but count each 'V' as one chain.

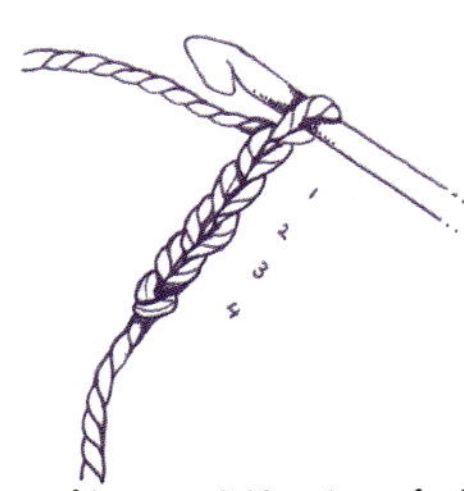

Making a slip stitch (sl st)

A slip stitch is used to join one stitch to another or a stitch to another point, as in joining a circle, and is usually made by picking up two strands of a stitch.

However, where it is worked into the starting chain, only pick up the back loop.

1. Insert the hook into the back loop of the next stitch and pass yarn over hook (yo), as in the chain stitch.

2. Draw yarn through both loops of stitch and repeat.

The magic ring: working in the round

There are two ways to start circular crochet. One is with a chain and another is with a loop. A loop, or magic ring, is the more usual way to make amigurumi. This way of working in the round ensures that there is no hole in the middle of the work, as there is with a chain ring, because the central hole is adjustable and can be pulled tightly closed.

Let's make a magic ring

This will be the first round of your amigurumi, so you need to master it!

1. Make a loop by wrapping the yarn twice onto your forefinger, with the tail end of the yarn on the right, the ball end on the left.

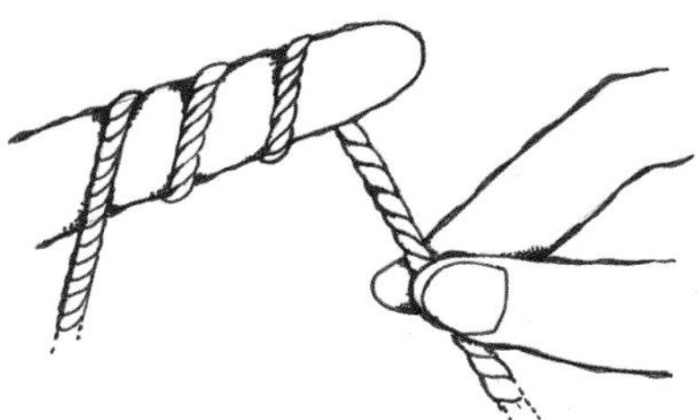

2. Pull the ball end through the loop (steady your work with your hand).

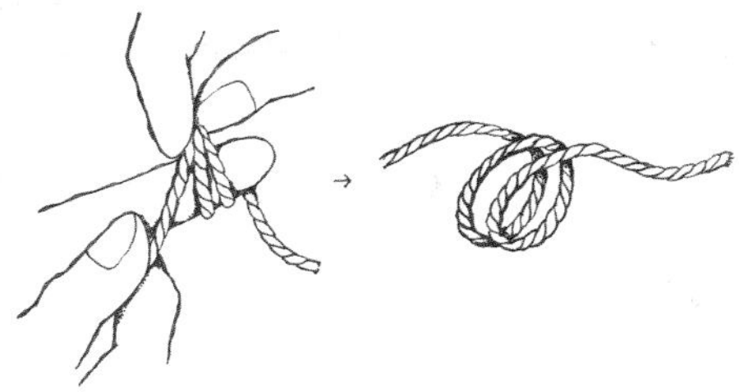

3. Make one chain (ch) through the loop on the hook you have drawn through to steady the round.

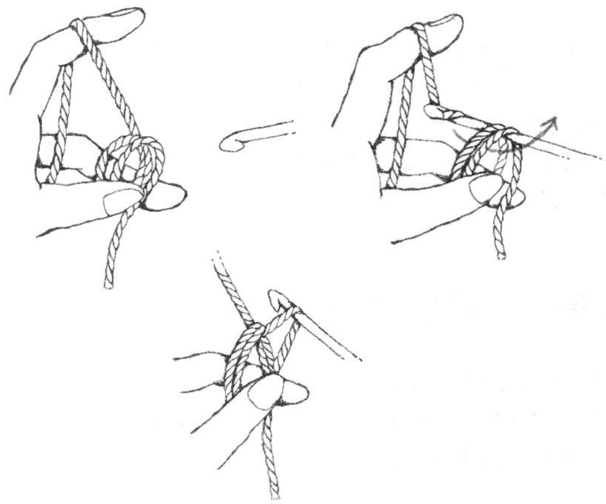

4. Work as many double crochet (dc), or whatever stitch you are using, into the loop as is required by the pattern.

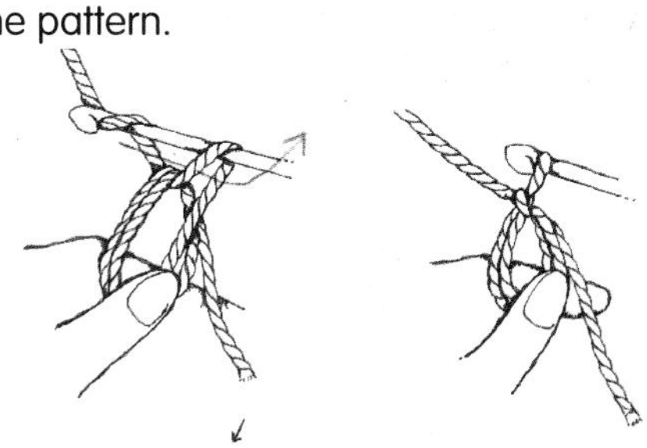

5. Pull the last stitch out long enough so that it won't come undone. Find out which loop will be tightened first by pulling one of the loops.

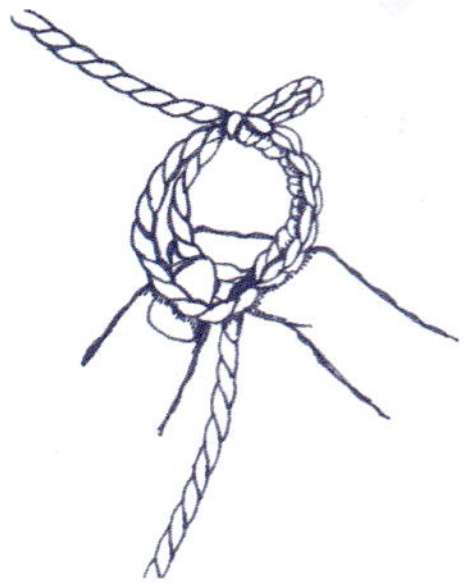

6. Pull this loop as tight as you can.

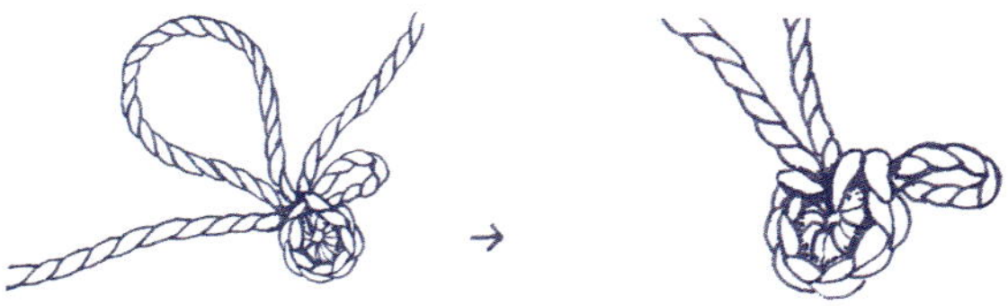

7. Pull the tail end of the yarn to tighten up the whole loop. Now you have no hole in the middle of the first round.

Completing the magic ring: first round

Insert the hook into the first stitch of a magic ring and pull the yarn through all the way.

This is called 'slip stitch' (sl st).

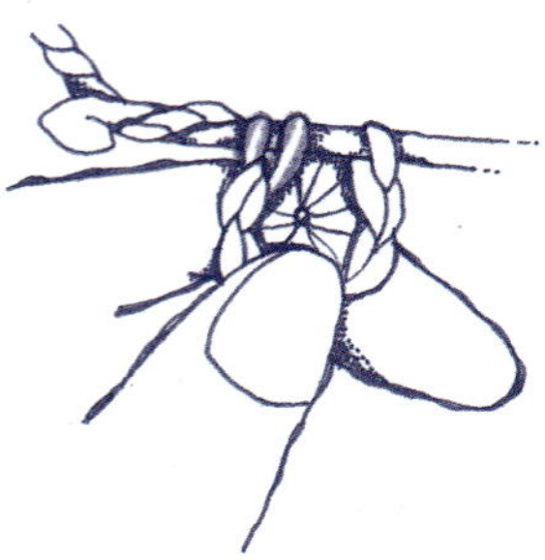

Start the second round

To crochet a flat circle, you need to keep working in the round with increasing stitches.

1. Make one chain (ch). Insert the hook into the first stitch of a circle, and put the yarn over the hook (yo) and then draw the yarn through the loop. This is called double crochet (dc). In amigurumi, this is the technique you will use the most.

2. Add one more dc into the same stitch. This is called increasing (inc).

Repeat 1 and 2 into every stitch and you will finish the second round with twice the number of stitches.

On the second round, increase in alternate stitches.

Third round: 1 dc into each of the next 2 stitches, 2 dc into the next one. Repeat.

Fourth round: 1 dc into each of the next 3 stitches, 2 dc into the next one. Repeat.

The more rounds you go, the more stitches you need to make between increases.

Making a chain ring

1. Work a chain as long as required by the pattern.
2. Join the last chain to the first with a slip stitch (sl st). Begin the first round by working into each chain stitch.

Variety of stitches

Double crochet (dc): the main stitch used for amigurumi

1. Insert the hook, front to back, into the next stitch. Yo.
2. Draw through one loop to front; there should be two loops on the hook. Yo.
3. Draw through both loops to complete double crochet.

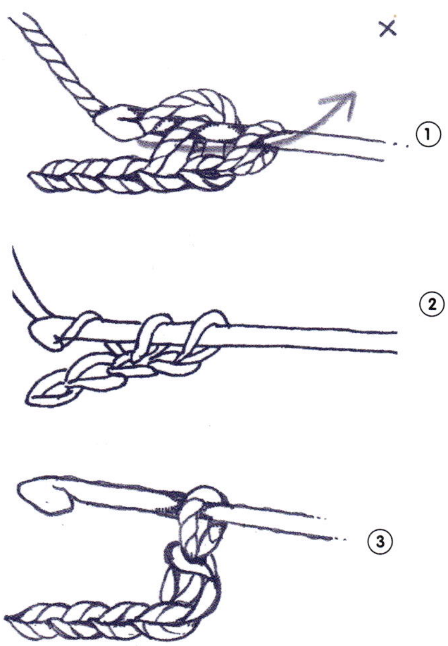

Treble crochet (tr)

This makes a more open fabric as the stitches are taller.

1. Wrap the yarn over the hook (yo) from back to front. Insert the hook into the next stitch, from front to back. Yo again and draw through the stitch.
2. There should be three loops on the hook. Yo and pull through two loops.
3. There should be two loops on the hook. Yo and pull through the remaining two loops.

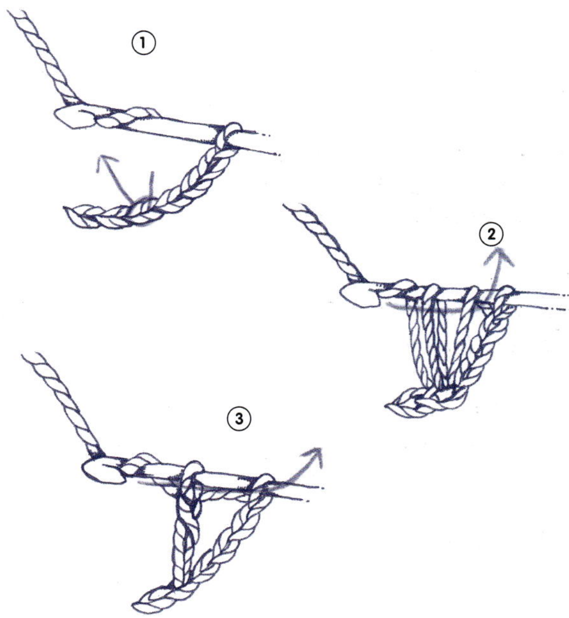

Half-treble crochet (htr)

The half-treble is simply that: half of a treble crochet. Therefore, the stitch is slightly shorter than treble crochet. In step 2 of treble crochet, pull through all the remaining loops in one movement.

Finishing Off

When you've finished crocheting your lovely presents, fastening off is the next most important step. After that, all you need to do is fill it with stuffing and stitch the parts together.

Here are some useful things to remember

When you fasten off the end of a part that is going to be stitched to another part, leave a long tail for sewing the two together. Do not weave this end in.

Connect two pieces by taking stitches alternately from each piece and fastening them securely.

Fastening off

1. After working the last stitch, snip off the yarn from the ball, leaving a length of a few centimetres to weave in.
2. Draw through the last loop, pulling tightly to fasten.

Weaving in ends

1. Use the hook to draw the yarn through at least five stitches, weaving the yarn over and under as you go to secure the yarn and ensure it does not work free.
2. Snip off the excess yarn.

When fastening off, leave openings for stuffing where appropriate. Stuff firmly, sew up gaps, and embroider details as shown in the illustrations.

Creating Happy Gifts

There aren't really any hard-and-fast rules when it comes to designing amigurumi. Once you've mastered the basic stitches and practised the technique of working in the round, you're bound to be inspired to start inventing your own crocheted creations. In this book you will find 25 patterns for all sorts of special events – from holidays to romantic occasions to birthdays and personal victories. But there are so many more special occasions out there to inspire you – so get out the crochet hook and start creating!

Developing a design

Amigurumi makes the perfect gift for any affair, and it can be easily adapted to suit your particular celebration.

Designs in this book are as diverse as a dragon to mark the Chinese New Year, Santa Claus and Rudolph the Red-Nose Reindeer, Love Birds for an anniversary (or just because) as well as ideas for a school graduation, but amigurumi isn't limited to these ideas alone. The best way to make your own one-of-a-kind design is to get inspired by browsing the internet or through books to find that one image that speaks to you – and then create it in crochet!

Don't be put off by my complicated designs – remember, you can make things in several parts and then stitch them all together later. And don't be afraid to try shapes other than round.

Sketching

When I have an idea, I start by making a sketch. It might be a pencil drawing or something more complicated, with colours added. You don't have to be good at drawing to do this; sometimes just a brief drawing of a shape and a little scribble of some details are enough to help you envisage the finished shape of your amigurumi, and to help you get started with the stitching.

Choosing materials

There are lots of lovely brightly coloured holiday motifs, so there is plenty of opportunity to get out some fun yarns. Bright greens, rosy reds and sunshine yellows can all make an appearance when celebrating our favourite occasions.

The choice of materials is endless. By playing with a variety of materials, you'll discover interesting differences in your finished result. Experiment with fancy yarns – yarns with touches of glitter and fluff – to create eye-catching textures.

Making shapes

This section will show you how to create some of the basic shapes for your projects. A lot of these shapes can be twisted and folded, or stitched to other shapes to create new ones.

Once you've mastered these, you can change the shapes to create all kinds of different celebratory objects.

Disc shapes

These are very simple to make. Start with the magic circle and then keep increasing stitches until the disc is the size you want. To make circular treats, make two discs, stitch together and stuff. To make semicircular items, fold a disc in half before stitching and stuffing.

Teardrop shapes

This type of shape is really simple. Just make a disc in the size you want, then continue with dc until the section is the length you require.

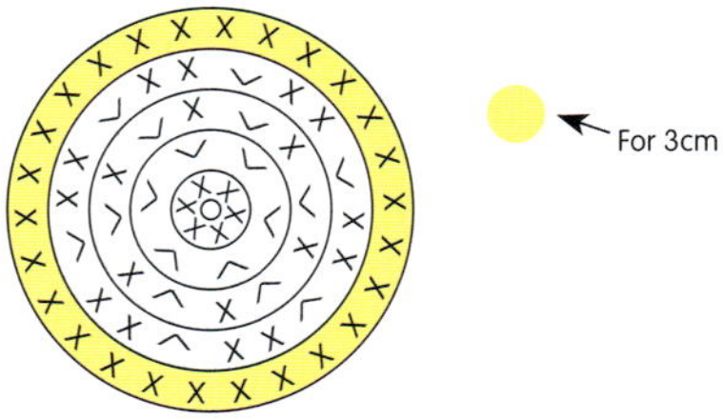

Ball shapes

Start with a disc shape, and then keep increasing stitches until the disc is the size of sphere you want to make. Continue for a couple of rounds without shaping, and then start decreasing.

Rectangles and squares

These are probably the easiest shapes to make. Start with a basic chain and then work crochet stitches along it. Turn the work at the end of the row and then work back along it. Keep going until you've got a piece the size you want. Squares and rectangles can be folded, bent or rolled into different shapes.

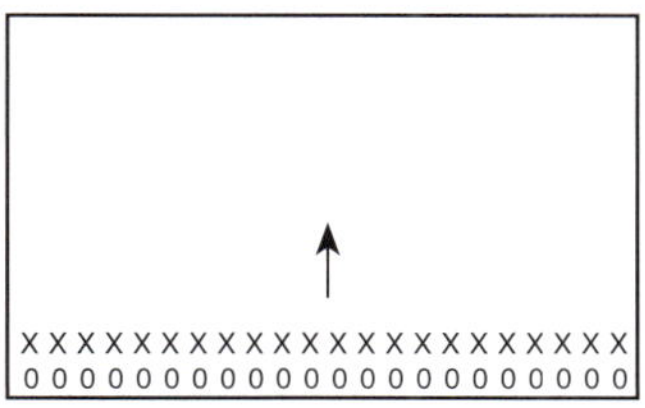

Rectangles with curved corners

To make this type of shape, start with a chain and work one row of stitches, just as for an ordinary square or rectangle. Then instead of turning the work and crocheting in rows, you work into the first chain, making stitches in the underside of the chain. To make sure the shape lies flat, you need to make at least three stitches in the first and last chains of the foundation chain.

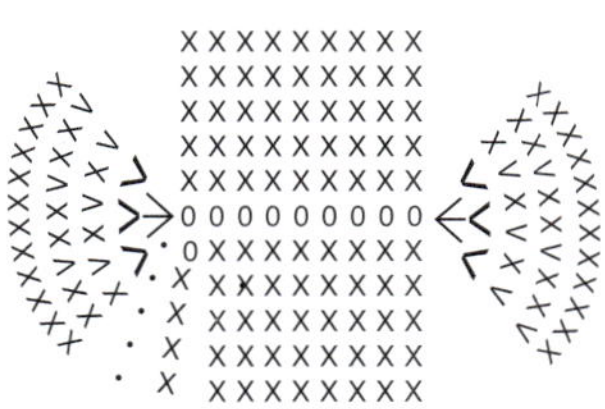

Rhomboid shapes

This four-sided shape looks like a sloping rectangle. It's useful for making twisted shapes. Start with a foundation chain as you would for a square or rectangle and then decrease by two stitches (dc2tog) at the beginning of the first row, and increase (2dc into same st) at the end of the row. On the next row, increase at the beginning and decrease at the end. Continue working, increasing and decreasing in the same way until the shape is as big as you need.

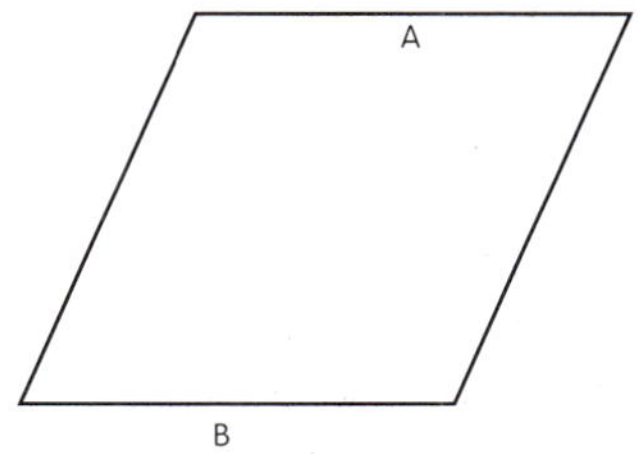

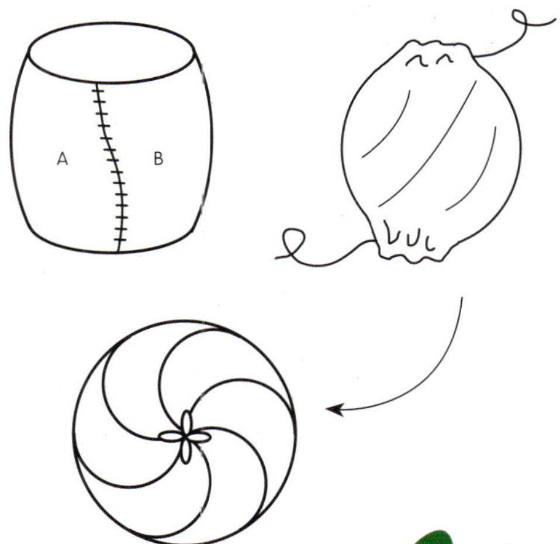

Chapter 1

Happy Holidays

Oh Christmas Tree!

Get the festivities started with a bit of special sparkle. Make a magical Christmas tree and deck its boughs with some shiny little baubles. Finish off this favourite decoration with a smiley super-star.

Size

Height with star: 16cm

Materials

HOOK SIZE: 3mm

YARN:

Green in different shades for the tree

Yellow for the star

Purple for the star faces

OTHER MATERIALS:

Toy filling

Small star-shaped beads for decoration

Gold ribbon or wrapping tape

Structure

The Christmas tree is made in three parts: the first is the tree, the second is the base, the third is frilly lengths, which are coiled around the base to represent the leaves.

Tree

Using green yarn, make a magic ring as follows.

Make a loop with tail end of yarn on right, keeping ball end on left. Pull the ball end through loop. Make one chain through loop on hook you have drawn through to steady the circle. Work 6dc into the circle and complete with sl st into the first dc. See also page 13.

1st round: 2dc into each dc. (12sts)

2nd–4th rounds: 1dc into each dc.

5th round: [1dc into next dc, 2dc into foll 1dc] 6 times. (18sts)

6th–8th rounds: 1dc into each dc.

9th round: [1dc into each of next 2dc, 2dc into foll 1dc] 6 times. (24sts)

10th–15th rounds: 1dc into each dc.

16th round: [1dc into each of next 3dc, 2dc into foll dc] 6 times. (30sts)

17th–22nd rounds: 1dc into each dc.

23rd round: [1dc into each of next 4dc, 2dc into foll dc] 6 times. (36sts)

24th–30th rounds: 1dc into each dc.

Fasten off.

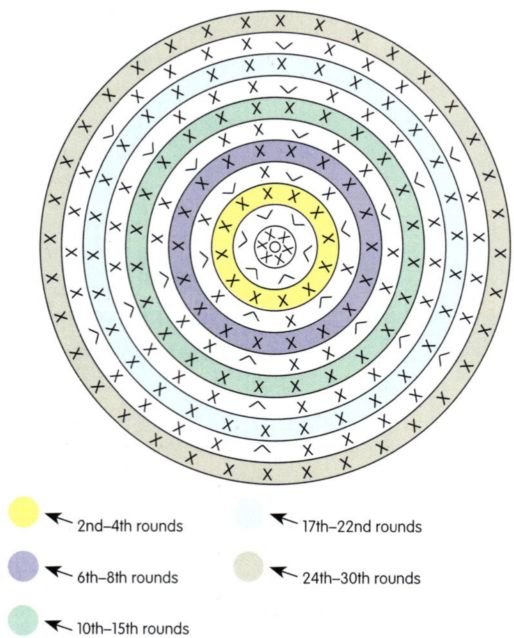

Base

Using green yarn, make a magic ring as for the tree.

1st round: 2dc into each dc. (12sts)

2nd round: [1dc into next dc, 2dc into foll 1dc] 6 times. (18sts)

3rd round: [1dc into each of next 2dc, 2dc into foll 1dc] 6 times. (24sts)

4th round: [1dc into each of next 3dc, 2dc into foll dc] 6 times. (30sts)

5th round: [1dc into each of next 4dc, 2dc into foll dc] 6 times. (36sts)

Fasten off.

Leaves

picot = 3ch, sl st into base of the 3ch just worked.

Using green yarn, make a ch a multiple of 4ch.

1st row: 1tr into the fourth ch from the hook, picot, 1tr into base of last tr, picot, *1ch, skip 1ch, 1dc into next ch, 1ch, skip 1ch, into next ch [1tr, picot] 5 times; repeat from * until 4ch remain, 1ch, skip 1ch, 1dc into next ch, 1ch, skip 1ch, into last ch [1tr, picot] 3 times.

Fasten off.

Repeat using different shades of green yarn worked to varying lengths.

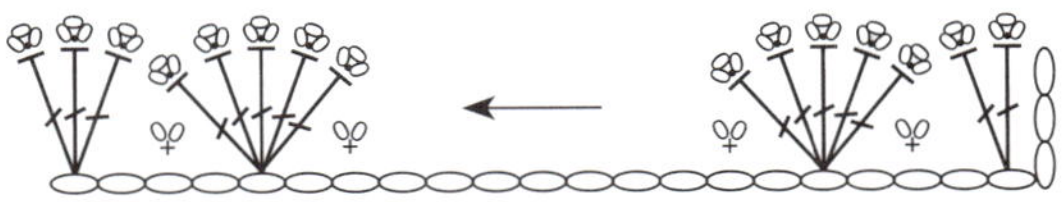

Star (make 2)

Using yellow yarn, make a magic ring as for the tree.

1st round: Working into the centre of the ring, [1dc, 2ch, 1tr, 2ch, 1dc] 4 times, 1dc, 2ch, 1tr, 2ch, sl st into first dc of the round.

2nd round: *1ch, skip 1ch, 1dc into next ch, [1dc, 1htr] into next tr, 2ch, 2dc into post of last htr, 1dc into the next ch, 1ch, sl st into next ch; repeat from * 4 times more.

Fasten off.

Making up

With your preferred side facing out and using matching yarn, sew the two pieces together around most of the outer edge, fill with toy stuffing and complete the seam. Then, using the photographs as reference, and purple yarn, embroider on cute faces!

Finishing

Pin the base to the tree and sew the two pieces together around most of the outer edge, fill with toy stuffing and complete the seam.

Using the photographs as reference and matching yarn, stitch the leaves and star to the tree. Decorate the tree with gold ribbon and small star-shaped beads to add Christmas magic.

Hello Santa

If you've been good, very-very good, then maybe this special Santa will pay you a visit. So don't forget to be on your best behaviour all year round if you want to see this jolly Christmas character.

Size

Height: 22cm

Materials

HOOK SIZE: 3mm

YARN:

Flesh-coloured for the head and nose

Cream for the hair, beard and bobble

Red for the cheeks, hat, arms, legs and body

Black for the belt

Yellow for the belt

OTHER MATERIALS:

Toy filling

2 toy safety eyes, 8mm

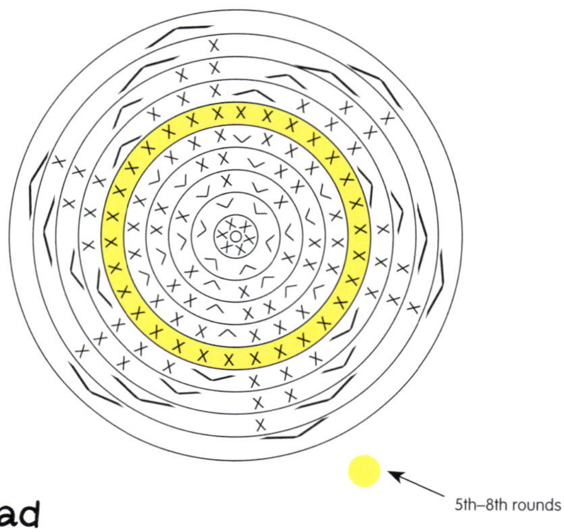

Head

Using flesh-coloured yarn, make a magic ring as follows.

Make a loop with tail end of yarn on right, keeping ball end on left. Pull the ball end through loop. Make one chain through loop on hook you have drawn through to steady the circle. Work 6dc into the circle and complete with sl st into the first dc. See also page 13.

1st round: 2dc into each dc. (12sts)

2nd round: [1dc into next dc, 2dc into foll 1dc] 6 times. (18sts)

3rd round: [1dc into each of next 2dc, 2dc into foll 1dc] 6 times. (24sts)

4th round: [1dc into each of next 3dc, 2dc into foll dc] 6 times. (30sts)

5th–8th rounds: 1dc into each dc.

9th round: [1dc into each of next 3dc, dc2tog] 6 times. (24sts)

10th round: [1dc into each of next 2dc, dc2tog] 6 times. (18sts)

Secure the toy safety eyes approximately 7sts apart on the sixth round and stuff the head with toy filling.

11th round: [1dc into next dc, dc2tog] 6 times. (12sts)

12th round: [dc2tog] 6 times. (6sts)

Fasten off.

Body

Using red yarn, make a magic ring as for the head.

1st round: 2dc into each dc. (12sts)

2nd round: [1dc into next dc, 2dc into foll dc] 6 times. (18sts)

3rd round: [1dc into each of next 2dc, 2dc into foll dc] 6 times. (24sts)

4th round: [1dc into each of next 3dc, 2dc into foll dc] 6 times. (30sts)

5th round: [1dc into each of next 4dc, 2dc into foll dc] 6 times. (36sts)

6th–10th rounds: 1dc into each dc.

11th round: [1dc into each of next 4dc, dc2tog] 6 times. (30sts)

12th round: 1dc into each dc.

13th round: [1dc into each of next 3dc, dc2tog] 6 times. (24sts)

14th round: 1dc into each dc.

15th round: [1dc into each of next 2dc, dc2tog] 6 times. (18sts)

16th round: 1dc into each dc.

17th round: [1dc into each of next 1dc, dc2tog] 6 times. (12sts)

Fasten off.

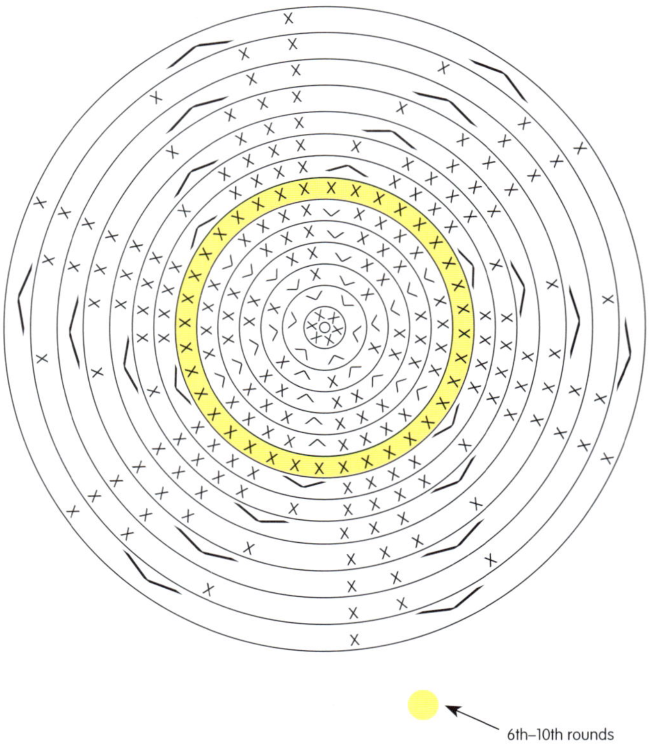

Nose

Using flesh-coloured yarn, make a magic ring as for the head.

1st round: 2dc into each dc. (12sts)

2nd–3rd rounds: 1dc into each dc.

Fasten off.

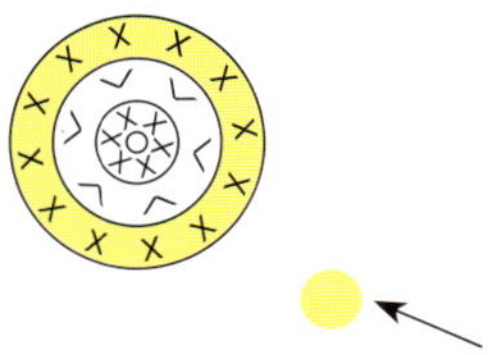

2nd–3rd rounds

Cheeks (make 2)

Using red yarn, make a magic ring as for the head.

Work as for nose.

Hair

Work each dc with long fur stitch loops worked as follows.

Insert the hook into the place or stitch directed, hook both sets of strands hanging down on either side of the raised index finger to create a loop, draw all the strands through the fabric, remove the index finger from the loop but hold the loop firmly against the fabric, wrap the yarn around the hook and draw it through all the loops on the hook. Firmly pull on the loop to draw it tight.

Using cream, make a magic ring as for the head.

1st round: 2dc into each dc. (12sts)

2nd round: [1dc into next dc, 2dc into foll dc] 6 times. (18sts)

3rd round: [1dc into each of next 2dc, 2dc into foll dc] 6 times. (24sts)

Fasten off.

Beard

Work each dc with long fur stitch loops worked as above for the hair.

Using cream yarn, make 6ch.

1st row: 1dc into the second ch from the hook, 1dc into each ch, turn. (5sts)

2nd–4th rows: 1ch, 1dc into each dc, turn.

Fasten off.

```
0XXXXX
 XXXXX0
 00000
```

Hat

Using red yarn, make a magic ring as for the head.

1st round: 1dc into each dc.

2nd round: 2dc into each dc. (12sts)

3rd–5th rounds: 1dc into each dc.

6th round: [1dc into next dc, 2dc into foll dc] 6 times. (18sts)

7th–8th rounds: 1dc into each dc.

Fasten off.

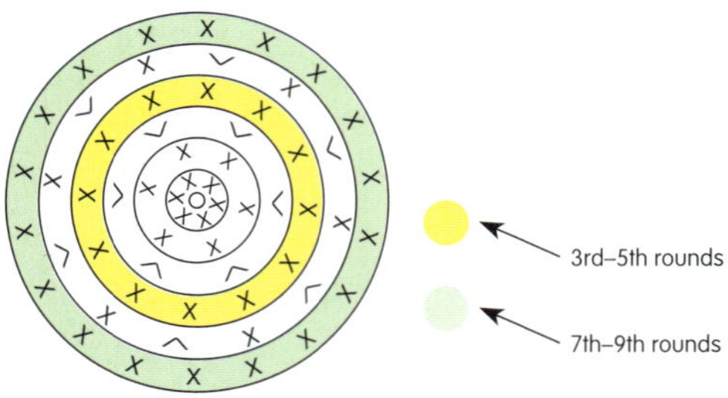

Hat bobble

Using cream yarn, make a magic ring as for the head.

1st–2nd rounds: 1dc into each dc.

Fasten off.

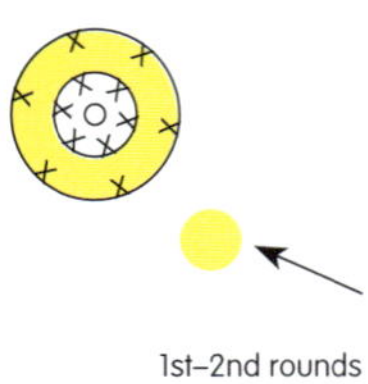

Legs (make 2)

Using red yarn, make a magic ring as for the head.

1st round: 2dc into each dc. (12sts)

2nd–7th rounds: 1dc into each dc.

Fasten off.

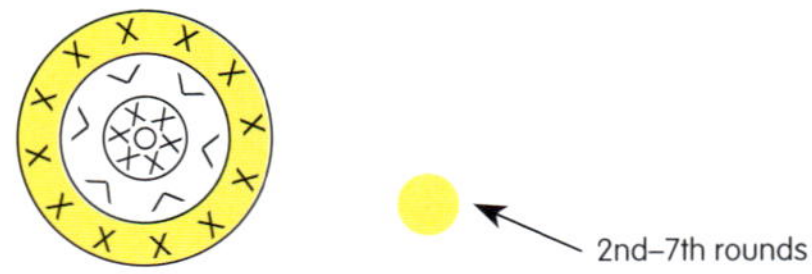

Arms (make 2)

Using red yarn, make a magic ring as for the head.

1st round: 2dc into each dc. (12sts)

2nd–10th rounds: 1dc into each dc.

Fasten off.

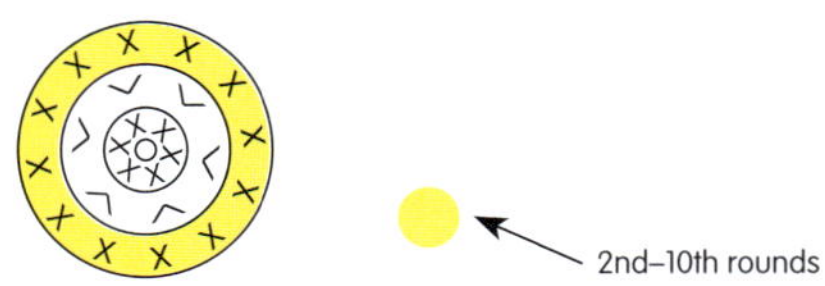

Making up

Using the photographs as reference and matching yarn, stitch the beard, cheeks and nose to the face and the hair and a hat stuff with toy filling to the head. Attach the bobble to the hat.

Stuff the body, arms and legs with toy filling. Attach the head, arms, and legs to the body.

To make the belt, using black yarn, make a ch long enough to go around the body.

1st row: 1dc into the second ch from the hook, 1dc into each ch, turn.

2nd row: 1ch, 1dc into each dc, turn.

Fasten off.

Using yellow yarn and straight stitches, embroider a buckle on to the belt.

Red-nose Reindeer

Santa wouldn't be able to do his gift-giving job without his happy helpers, and no one is more important than the reindeers that pull his sleigh. Crochet this cute red-nose critter to be your own special Christmas companion.

Size

Height: 21cm

Materials

HOOK SIZE: 3mm

YARN:

Brown for the head, ears, snout, jaw, chest, body legs and tail

Light brown for the antlers and feet

Red for the nose

OTHER MATERIALS:

Toy filling

2 toy safety eyes, 8mm

Structure

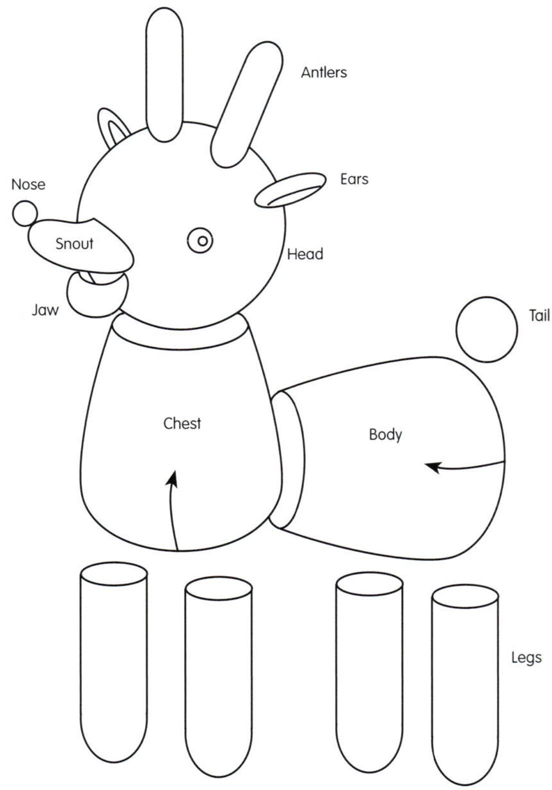

Head

Using brown yarn, make a magic ring as follows.

Make a loop with tail end of yarn on right, keeping ball end on left. Pull the ball end through loop. Make one chain through loop on hook you have drawn through to steady the circle. Work 6dc into the circle and complete with sl st into the first dc. See also page 13.

1st round: 2dc into each dc. (12sts)

2nd round: [1dc into next dc, 2dc into foll 1dc] 6 times. (18sts)

3rd round: [1dc into each of next 2dc, 2dc into foll 1dc] 6 times. (24sts)

4th round: [1dc into each of next 3dc, 2dc into foll dc] 6 times. (30sts)

5th–8th rounds: 1dc into each dc.

9th round: [1dc into each of next 3dc, dc2tog] 6 times. (24sts)

10th round: [1dc into each of next 2dc, dc2tog] 6 times. (18sts)

Secure the toy safety eyes approximately 6sts apart on the sixth round and stuff the head with toy filling.

11th round: [1dc into next dc, dc2tog] 6 times. (12sts)

12th round: [dc2tog] 6 times. (6sts)

Fasten off.

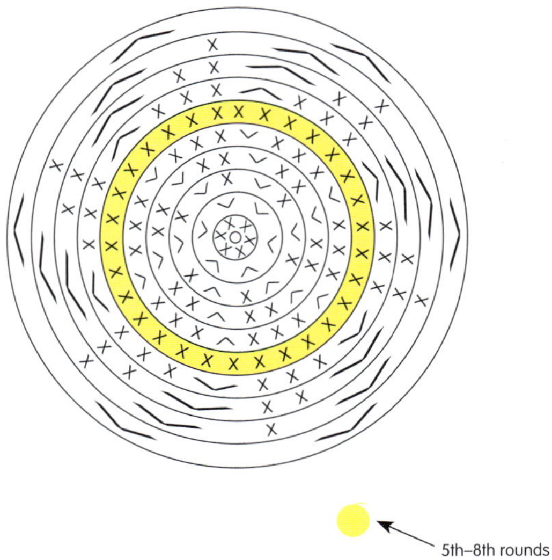

Chest

Using brown yarn, make a magic ring as for the head.

1st round: 2dc into each dc. (12sts)

2nd round: [1dc into next dc, 2dc into foll dc] 6 times. (18sts)

3rd round: [1dc into each of next 2dc, 2dc into foll dc] 6 times. (24sts)

4th round: [1dc into each of next 3dc, 2dc into foll dc] 6 times. (30sts)

5th–9th rounds: 1dc into each dc.

10th round: [1dc into each of next 3dc, dc2tog] 6 times. (24sts)

11th round: 1dc into each dc.

12th round: [1dc into each of next 2dc, dc2tog] 6 times. (18sts)

13th–14th rounds: 1dc into each dc.

Fasten off.

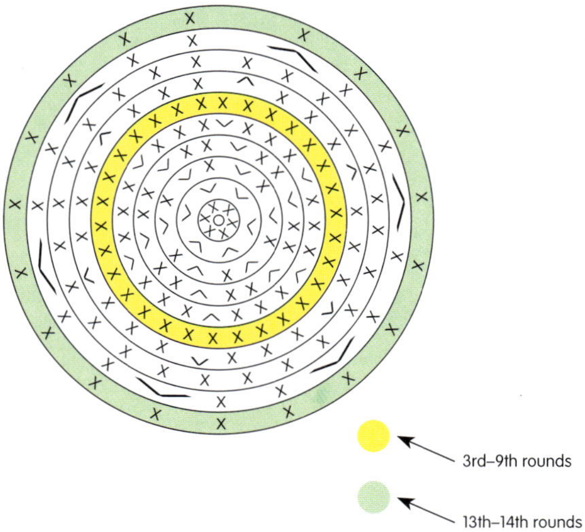

Body

Using brown yarn, make a magic ring as for the head.

1st round: 2dc into each dc. (12sts)

2nd round: [1dc into next dc, 2dc into foll dc] 6 times. (18sts)

3rd round: [1dc into each of next 2dc, 2dc into foll dc] 6 times. (24sts)

5th–9th rounds: 1dc into each dc.

Fasten off.

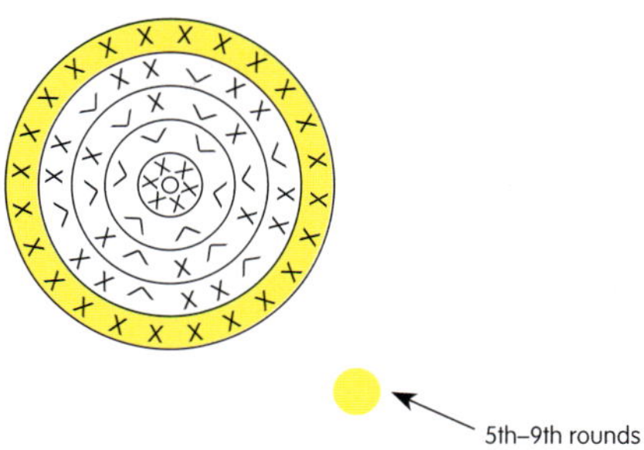

Legs (make 4)

Using light brown yarn, make a magic ring as for the head.

1st round: 2dc into each dc. (12sts)

2nd–4th rounds: 1dc into each dc.

Fasten off light brown yarn, join in brown.

5nd–12th rounds: 1dc into each dc.

Fasten off.

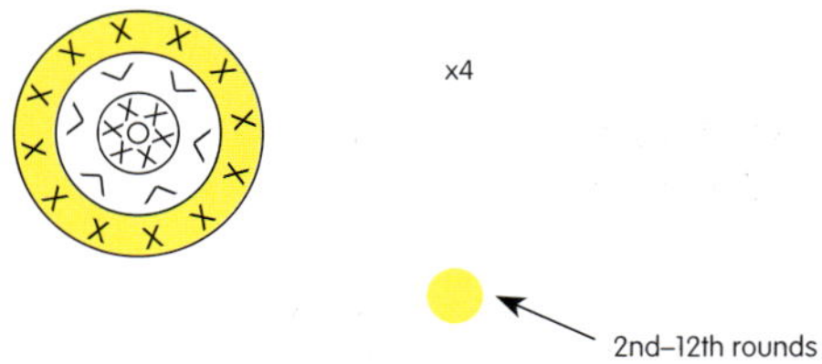

Snout

Using brown yarn, make a magic ring as for the head.

1st round: 2dc into each dc. (12sts)

2nd–4th rounds: 1dc into each dc.

5th round: [1dc into next dc, 2dc into foll dc] 6 times. (18sts)

6th–7th rounds: 1dc into each dc.

Fasten off.

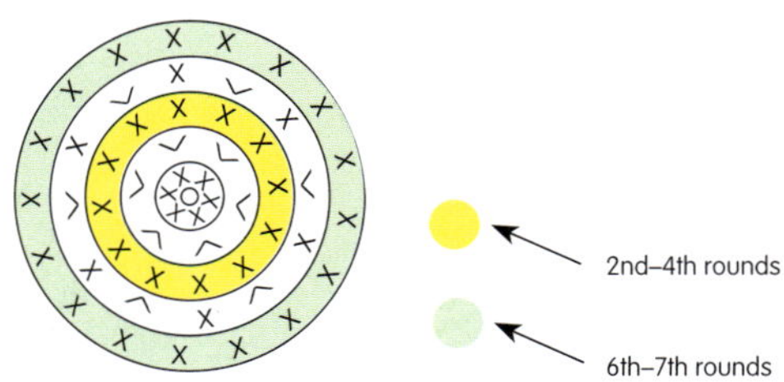

Nose

Using red yarn, make a magic ring as for the head.

1st round: 2dc into each dc. (12sts)

2nd–4th rounds: 1dc into each dc.

Fasten off.

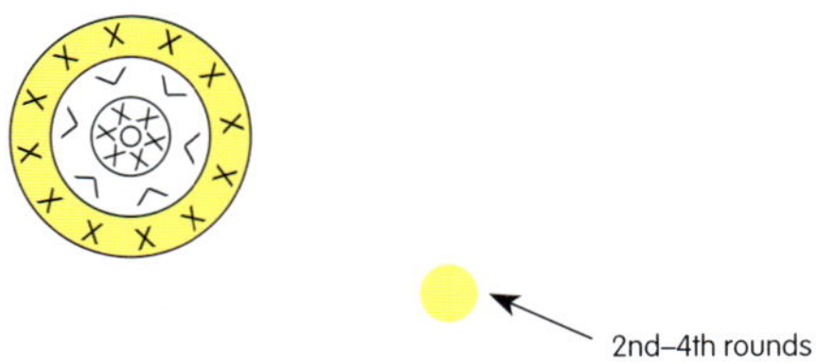

Mouth

Using brown yarn, make a magic ring as for the head.

1st round: 2dc into each dc. (12sts)

2nd round: [1dc into next dc, 2dc into foll dc] 6 times. (18sts)

3rd–4th rounds: 1dc into each dc.

Fasten off.

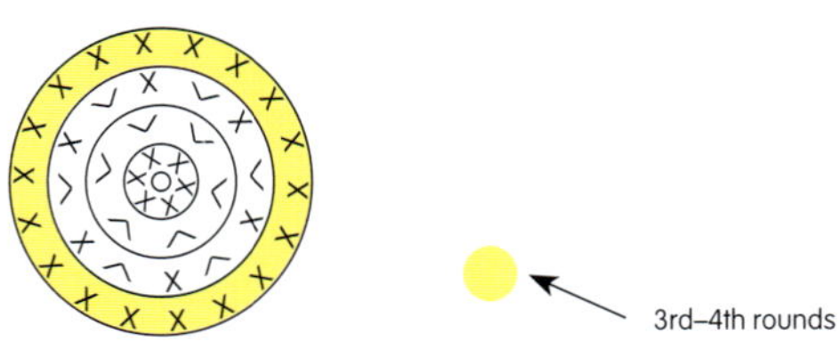

Ears (make 2)

Using brown yarn, make a magic ring as for the head.

1st round: 2dc into each dc. (12sts)

2nd round: [1dc into next dc, 2dc into foll dc] 6 times. (18sts)

Fasten off.

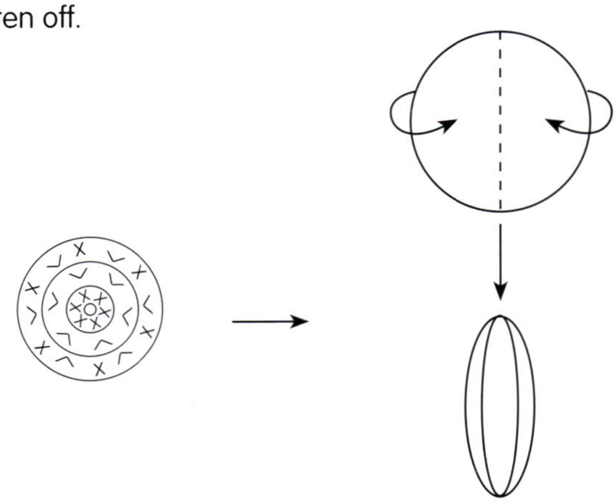

Antlers (make 2)

Using light brown yarn, make a magic ring as for the head.

1st–8th rounds: 1dc into each dc.

Fasten off.

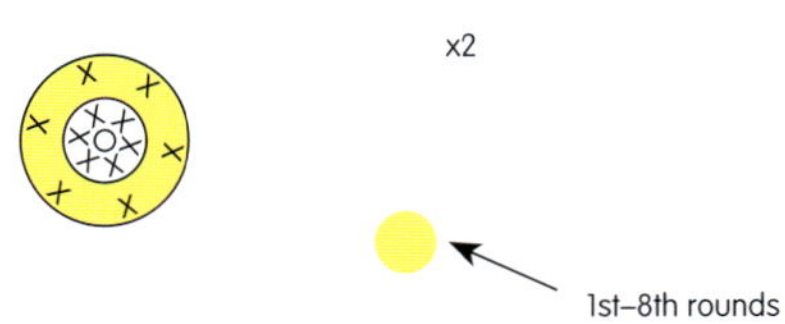

Tail

Using brown yarn, make a magic ring as for the head.

1st round: 2dc into each dc. (12sts)

2nd–5th rounds: 1dc into each dc.

Fasten off.

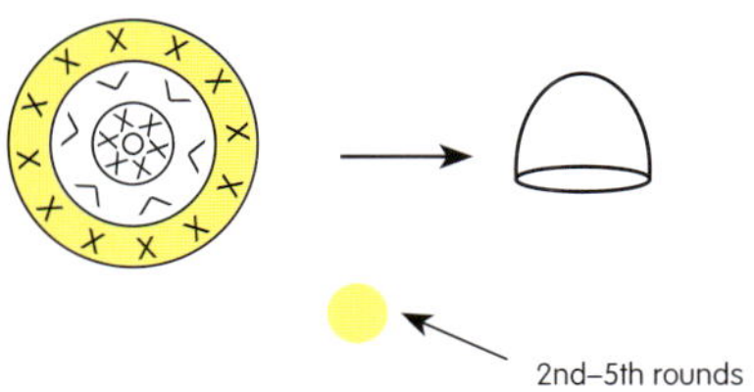

Making up

Stuff the head, snout and nose with toy filling. Sew nose to snout. Pinch a small section of each ear piece and stitch in place. Using the photographs as reference and matching yarn, stitch the antlers, ears snout, mouth and nose to the head. Stuff the chest, body and legs with toy filling.

Attach the head and body to the chest. Pin the legs to the body and chest sections and adjust their position as required in order for the reindeer to stand. Stitch the legs in place and attach the tail.

Angel Girl

Hark the happy angels sing! It's Christmas time! This glittery angel girl is sure to brighten up anyone's yuletide celebrations. Pop her on the tree and she can outshine all the other decorations.

Size

Height: 20cm

Materials

HOOK SIZE: 3mm

YARN:

Flesh-coloured for the head and nose

White and cream for the body

Cream for the legs

Blue Lurex or sparkly yarn for the cape and halo.

Red for the cheeks

Yellow for the hair

OTHER MATERIALS:

Toy filling

2 toy safety eyes, 8mm

Structure

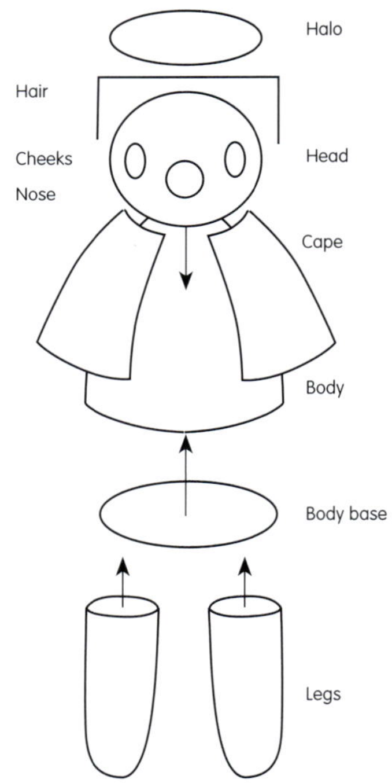

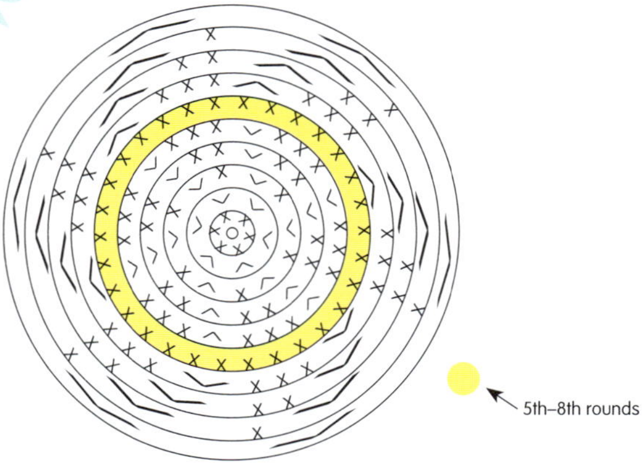

Head

Using flesh-coloured yarn, make a magic ring as follows.

Make a loop with tail end of yarn on right, keeping ball end on left. Pull the ball end through loop. Make one chain through loop on hook you have drawn through to steady the circle. Work 6dc into the circle and complete with sl st into the first dc. See also page 13.

1st round: 2dc into each dc. (12sts)

2nd round: [1dc into next dc, 2dc into foll 1dc] 6 times. (18sts)

3rd round: [1dc into each of next 2dc, 2dc into foll 1dc] 6 times. (24sts)

4th round: [1dc into each of next 3dc, 2dc into foll dc] 6 times. (30sts)

5th–8th rounds: 1dc into each dc.

9th round: [1dc into each of next 3dc, dc2tog] 6 times. (24sts)

10th round: [1dc into each of next 2dc, dc2tog] 6 times. (18sts)

Secure the toy safety eyes approximately 6sts apart on the sixth round and stuff the head with toy filling.

11th round: [1dc into next dc, dc2tog] 6 times. (12sts)

12th round: [dc2tog] 6 times. (6sts)

Fasten off.

Body

Using white and cream yarn stranded together, make a magic ring as for the head.

1st round: 2dc into each dc. (12sts)

2nd round: [1dc into next dc, 2dc into foll dc] 6 times. (18sts)

3rd round: [1dc into each of next 2dc, 2dc into foll dc] 6 times. (24sts)

4th round: [1dc into each of next 3dc, 2dc into foll dc] 6 times. (30sts)

5th–14th rounds: 1dc into each dc.

Fasten off.

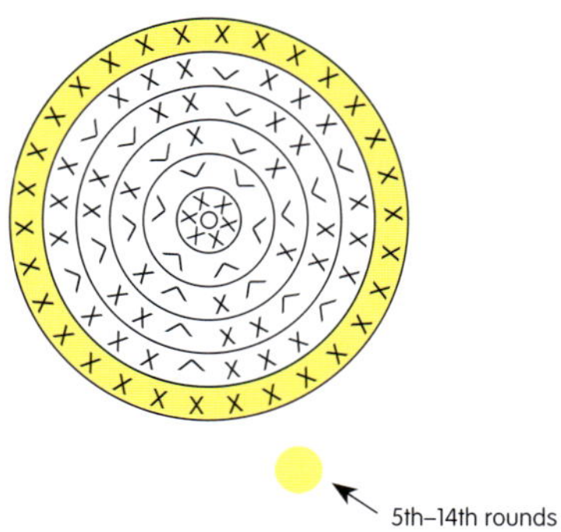

Body base

Using cream yarn, make a magic ring as for the head.

1st round: 2dc into each dc. (12sts)

2nd round: [1dc into next dc, 2dc into foll dc] 6 times. (18sts)

3rd round: [1dc into each of next 2dc, 2dc into foll dc] 6 times. (24sts)

4th round: [1dc into each of next 3dc, 2dc into foll dc] 6 times. (30sts)

5th round: 1dc into each dc.

Fasten off.

Legs (make 2)

Using cream yarn, make a magic ring as for the head.

1st round: 2dc into each dc. (12sts)

2nd round: [1dc into next dc, 2dc into foll dc] 6 times. (18sts)

Work 1dc into each dc until the piece measures 5cm.

Fasten off.

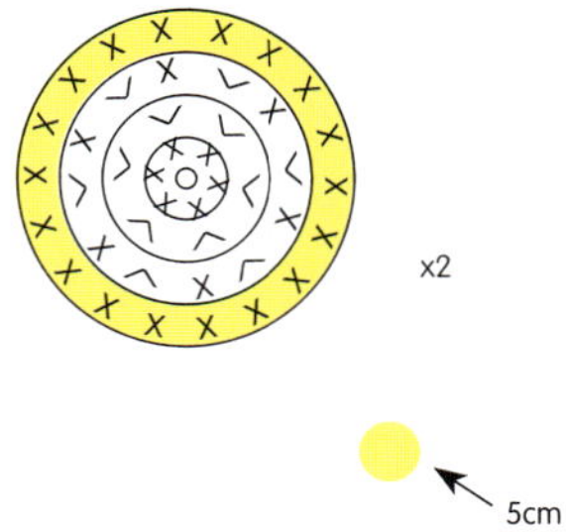

Cheeks (make 2)

Using red yarn, make a magic ring as for the head.

Fasten off.

Nose

Using flesh-coloured yarn, make a magic ring as for the Head.

1st–2nd rounds: 1dc into each dc. (6sts)

Fasten off.

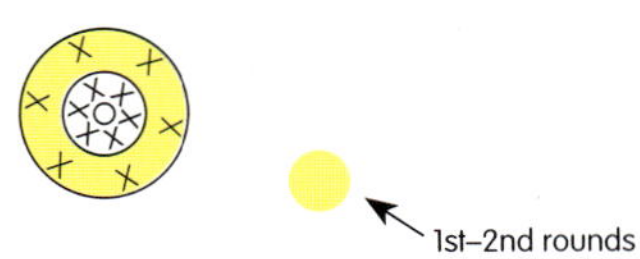

Cape

Using blue Lurex yarn, make 30ch.

1st row: 1dc into the eleventh ch from the hook, [5ch, skip 3ch, 1dc into next ch] 4 times, 3ch, 1tr into last ch, turn.

2nd row: 7ch, skip ch-sp, 1dc into next ch-sp, [5ch, skip 3ch, 1dc into next ch] 4 times, 3ch, 1tr into the same ch-sp as last dc, turn.

Repeat the last row three more times.

Fasten off.

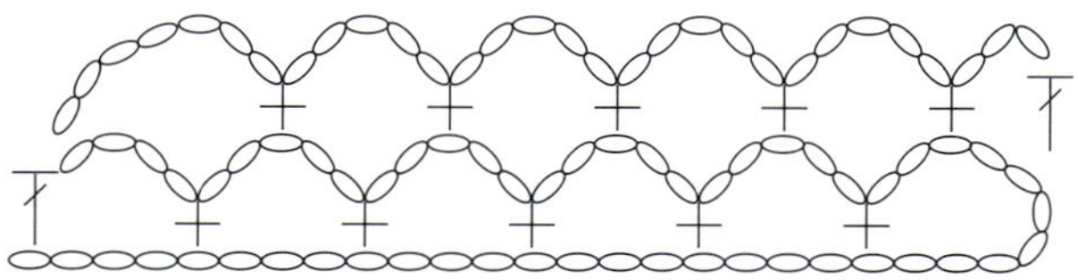

Halo

2tr-bobble = [wrap the yarn around the hook, insert the hook into fourth ch from hook, wrap yarn around hook, draw yarn through ch, wrap yarn around hook, draw yarn through two loops on hook] twice, wrap yarn around hook draw yarn through all loops on the hook.

Using blue Lurex yarn, make 4ch.

1st row: 2tr-bobble, [4ch, 2tr-bobble] 9 times.

Fasten off.

Making up

Using the photographs as reference and matching yarn, stitch the cheeks and nose to the face.

To make hair, wrap yellow yarn around a piece of cardboard 14cm wide, approximately ten times, secure with a loop of matching yarn and leave long yarn-ends for sewing to the head. Fold each section in half and attach to the head.

Attach the halo, allowing some hair to appear to be covering the halo.

Using the structure diagram and photographs as reference, stuff and assemble the body and leg pieces.

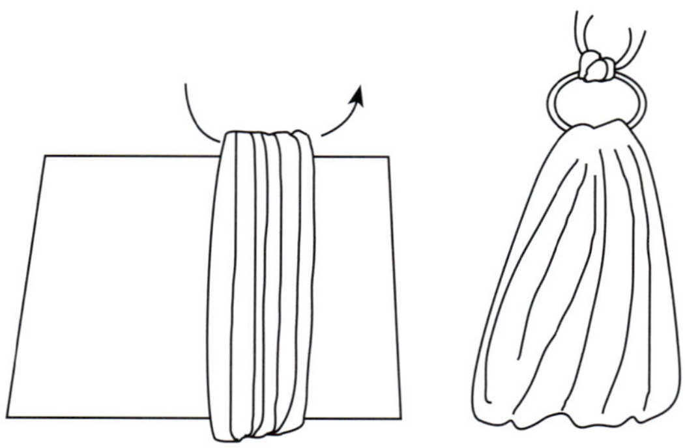

Wow Wow Candles

Let in the light and illuminate your winter celebrations with these cheery candles. Set them on the festive table and they will shine and shimmer throughout the dark nights. Happy Hanukkah!

Size

Heights: 11cm; 13.5cm; 16cm

Materials

HOOK size: 3mm

YARN:

White for the wax

Red for the flame

OTHER MATERIALS:

Cardboard

Toy filling

3rd round onwards until the desired height is reached

Candle body

Make candles of three different heights (for your menorah make x3 sets)!

Using white yarn, make a magic ring as follows.

Make a loop with tail end of yarn on right, keeping ball end on left. Pull the ball end through loop. Make one chain through loop on hook you have drawn through to steady the circle. Work 6dc into the circle and complete with sl st into the first dc. See also page 13.

1st round: 2dc into each dc. (12sts)

2nd round: [1dc into next dc, 2dc into foll 1dc] 6 times. (18sts)

3rd round: 1dc into each dc.

Repeat the last round until the desired height is reached.

Fasten off.

Candle body base

Using white yarn, make a magic ring as for the candle body.

1st round: 2dc into each dc. (12sts)

2nd round: [1dc into next dc, 2dc into foll dc] 6 times. (18sts)

Fasten off.

Wax collar

Using white yarn, make a magic ring as for the candle body.

1st round: 2dc into each dc. (12sts)

2nd round: [1dc into next dc, 2dc into foll dc] 6 times. (18sts)

3rd round: Work ch lengths and, dc, htr and tr sts, randomly for melting wax effect.

Flame

Using red yarn, make a magic ring as for the candle body.

1st round: 2dc into each dc. (12sts)

2nd round: [1dc into next dc, 2dc into foll 1dc] 6 times. (18sts)

3rd–5th rounds: 1dc into each dc.

6th round: [1dc into next dc, dc2tog] 6 times. (12sts)

7th round: [dc2tog] 6 times. (6sts)

Fasten off.

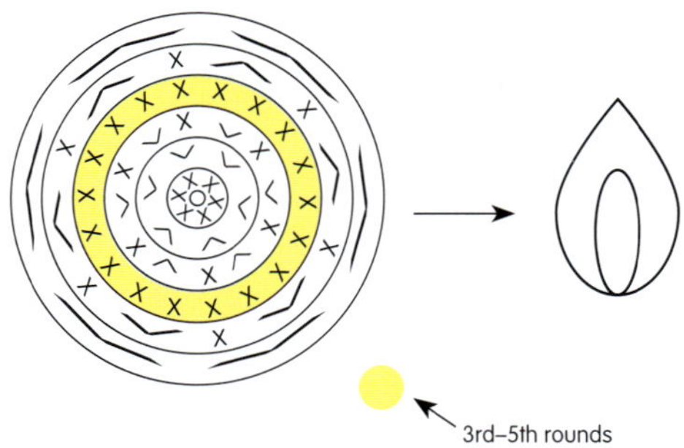

Making up

Cut the cardboard to the same length as the candle body and roll it into a cylinder shape. Insert the cardboard roll and toy filling into the candle body.

Using the photographs on page 43 as reference and matching yarn, stitch the candle body base, the wax collar, an unstuffed flame to the candle body.

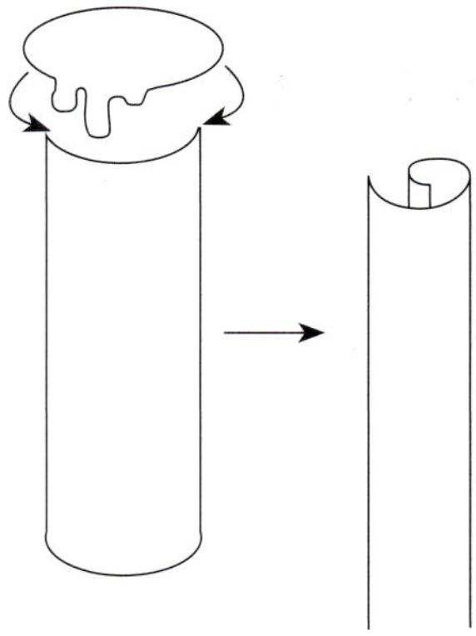

Thanksgiving Turkey

As leaves turn gold and start to fall, it's the traditional time to celebrate the end of summer goodness. This trim little turkey is the perfect guest at any feast and makes the ideal gift to say a special thank you to best friends.

Size

Height: 11cm

Materials

HOOK SIZE: 3mm

YARN:

Brown for the head and body

Yellow for the beak and tail

Red for wattle and tail

OTHER MATERIALS:

Toy filling

2 toy safety eyes, 8mm

Structure

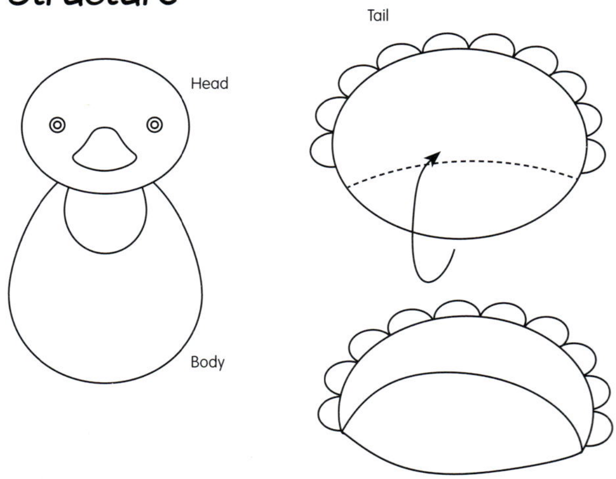

Head

Using brown yarn, make a magic ring as follows.

Make a loop with tail end of yarn on right, keeping ball end on left. Pull the ball end through loop. Make one chain through loop on hook you have drawn through to steady the circle. Work 6dc into the circle and complete with sl st into the first dc. See also page 13.

1st round: 2dc into each dc. (12sts)

2nd round: [1dc into next dc, 2dc into foll 1dc] 6 times. (18sts)

3rd round: [1dc into each of next 2dc, 2dc into foll 1dc] 6 times. (24sts)

4th–7th rounds: 1dc into each dc.

8th round: [1dc into each of next 2dc, dc2tog] 6 times. (18sts)

Secure the toy safety eyes approximately 4sts apart on the sixth round and stuff the head with toy filling.

9th round: [1dc into next dc, dc2tog] 6 times. (12sts)

10th round: [dc2tog] 6 times. (6sts)

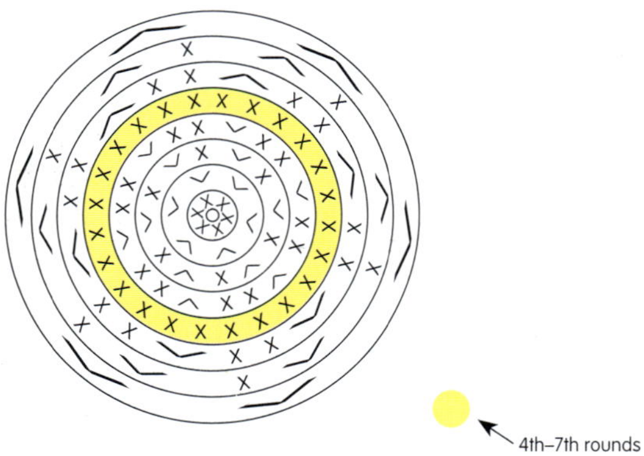

Body

Using brown yarn, make a magic ring as for the head.

1st round: 2dc into each dc. (12sts)

2nd round: [1dc into next dc, 2dc into foll dc] 6 times. (18sts)

3rd round: [1dc into each of next 2dc, 2dc into foll dc] 6 times. (24sts)

4th–7th rounds: 1dc into each dc.

8th round: [1dc into each of next 2dc, dc2tog] 6 times. (18sts)

9th–11th rounds: 1dc into each dc.

12th round: [1dc into next dc, dc2tog] 6 times. (12sts)

13th round: 1dc into each dc.

Fasten off.

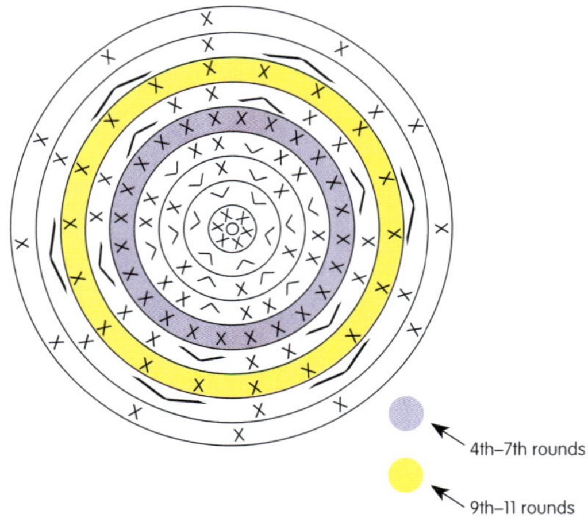

Tail

Using red yarn double stranded, make a magic ring as for the head.

1st round: 2dc into each dc. (12sts)

2nd round: [1dc into next dc, 2dc into foll dc] 6 times. (18sts)

3rd round: [1dc into each of next 2dc, 2dc into foll dc] 6 times. (24sts)

4th round: [1dc into each of next 3dc, 2dc into foll dc] 6 times. (30sts)

5th round: [1dc into each of next 4dc, 2dc into foll dc] 6 times. (36sts)

Fasten off red yarn, join in yellow yarn.

6th round: *1dc into next dc, into the foll stitch [1htr, 3tr, 1htr]; repeat from * 9 more times, 1dc into the next dc.

Fasten off.

Beak

Using yellow yarn, make a magic ring as for the head.

1st round: 2dc into each dc. (12sts)

2nd–4th rounds: 1dc into each dc.

Fasten off.

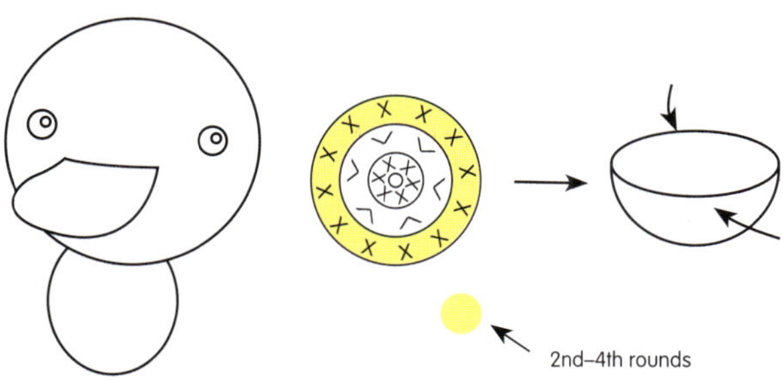

Wattle

Using red yarn, make a magic ring as for the head.

1st round: 2dc into each dc. (12sts)

2nd round: [1dc into next dc, 2dc into foll dc] 6 times. (18sts)

3rd–6th rounds: 1dc into each dc.

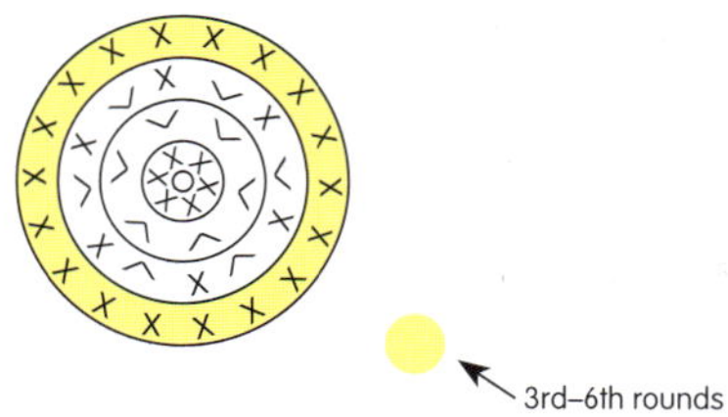

Making up

Using the structure diagram and photographs as reference and matching yarn, stuff and assemble the body and head pieces. Attach the beak and wattle to the face. Fold the tail as shown in the structure diagram and attach to the body.

New Year Dragon

Red is the colour of good fortune in China and New Year is the time to give presents. So ensure you have a lucky year ahead and make this friendly beast to welcome in the Year of the Dragon!

Size

Height: 13cm

Materials

HOOK SIZE: 3mm

YARN:

Red for the head, nose, neck, body and tail

Yellow for the arms, legs, feet and spine

Green for the ears

OTHER MATERIALS:

Toy filling

2 toy safety eyes, 8mm

Structure

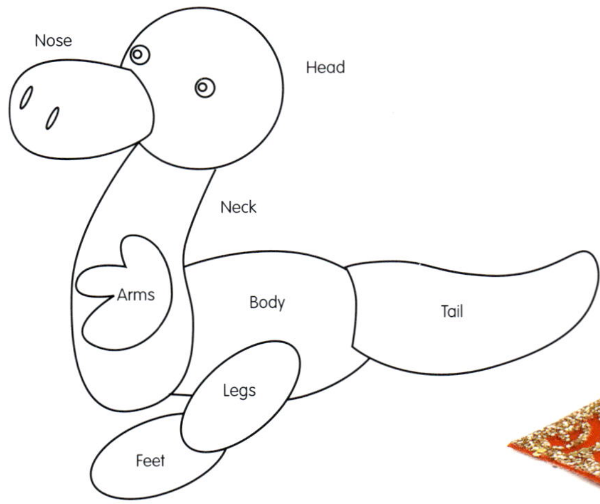

Head

Using red yarn, make a magic ring as follows.

Make a loop with tail end of yarn on right, keeping ball end on left. Pull the ball end through loop. Make one chain through loop on hook you have drawn through to steady the circle. Work 6dc into the circle and complete with sl st into the first dc. See also page 13.

1st round: 2dc into each dc. (12sts)

2nd round: [1dc into next dc, 2dc into foll 1dc] 6 times. (18sts)

3rd round: [1dc into each of next 2dc, 2dc into foll 1dc] 6 times. (24sts)

4th–7th rounds: 1dc into each dc.

8th round: [1dc into each of next 2dc, dc2tog] 6 times. (18sts)

Secure the toy safety eyes approximately 5sts apart on the third round and stuff the head with toy filling.

9th round: [1dc into next dc, dc2tog] 6 times. (12sts)

10th round: [dc2tog] 6 times. (6sts)

Fasten off.

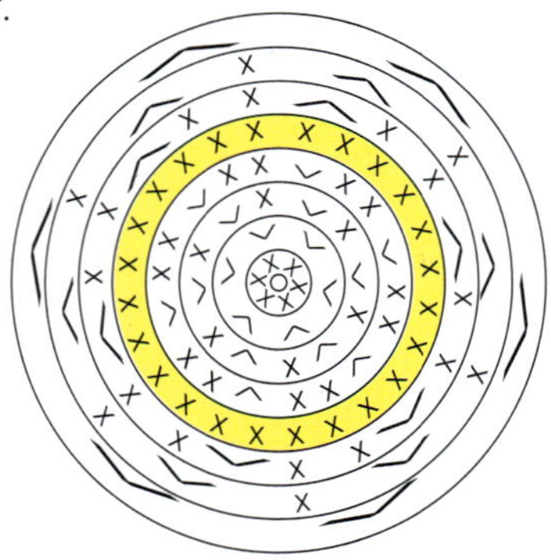

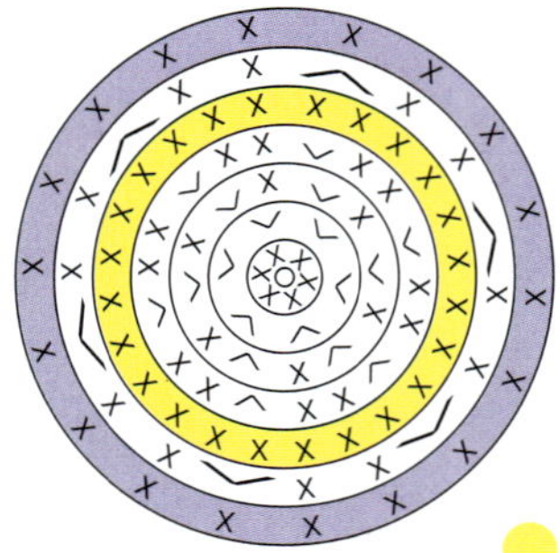

Nose

Using red yarn, make a magic ring as for the head.

1st round: 2dc into each dc. (12sts)

2nd round: [1dc into next dc, 2dc into foll dc] 6 times. (18sts)

3rd round: [1dc into each of next 2dc, 2dc into foll dc] 6 times. (24sts)

4th–6th rounds: 1dc into each dc.

7th round: [1dc into each of next 2dc, dc2tog] 6 times. (18sts)

8th–9th rounds: 1dc into each dc.

Fasten off.

Neck

Using red yarn, make a magic ring as for the head.

1st round: 2dc into each dc. (12sts)

2nd round: [1dc into next dc, 2dc into foll dc] 6 times. (18sts)

3rd–20th rounds: 1dc into each dc.

Fasten off

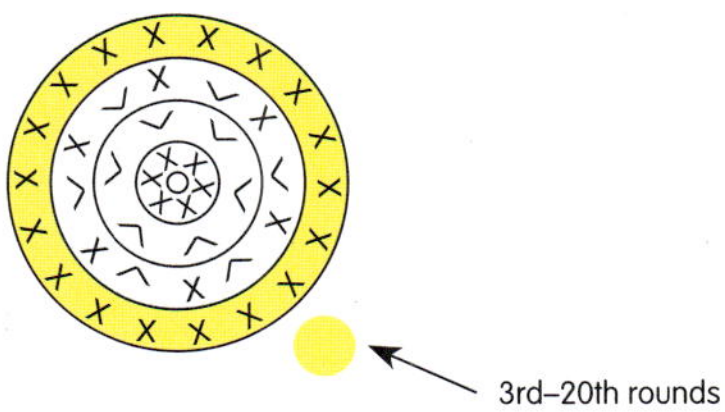

Body

Using red yarn, make a magic ring as for the head.

1st round: 2dc into each dc. (12sts)

2nd round: [1dc into next dc, 2dc into foll dc] 6 times. (18sts)

3rd–10th rounds: 1dc into each dc.

Fasten off.

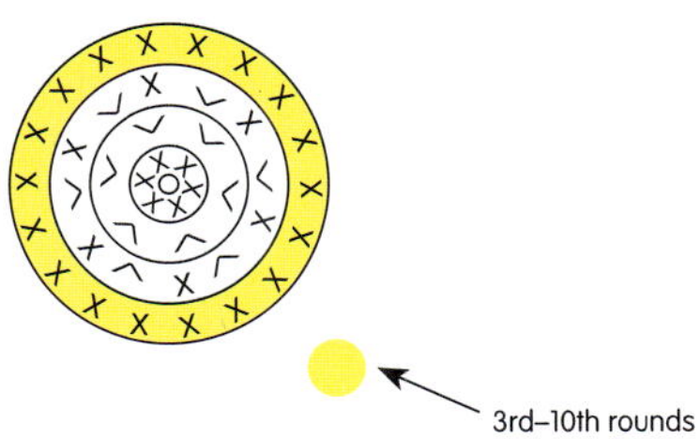

Tail

Using red yarn, make a magic ring as for the head.

1st round: 2dc into each dc. (12sts)

2nd–5th rounds: 1dc into each dc.

6th round: [1dc into next dc, 2dc into foll dc] 6 times. (18sts)

7th–16th rounds: 1dc into each dc.

Fasten off.

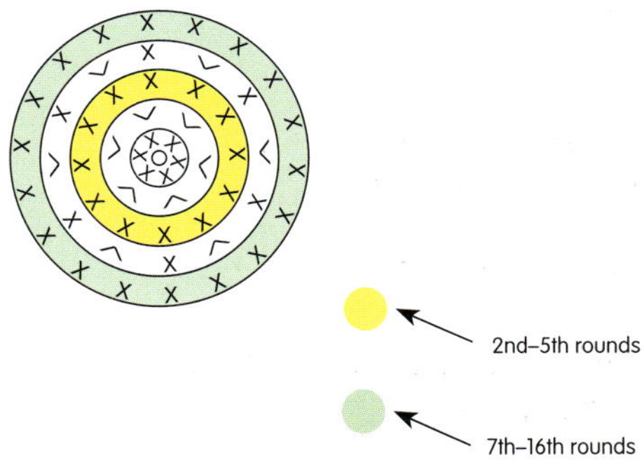

Legs (make 2)

Using yellow yarn, make a magic ring as for the head.

1st round: 2dc into each dc. (12sts)

3rd–8th rounds: 1dc into each dc.

Fasten off.

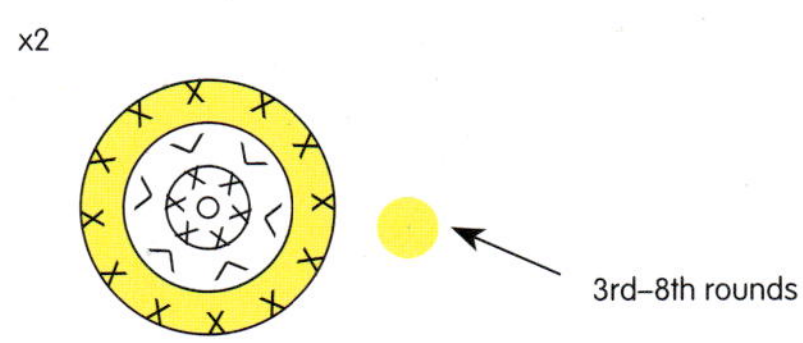

Feet (make 2)

Using yellow yarn, make a magic ring as for the head.

1st round: 2dc into each dc. (12sts)

~~3rd~~ 2nd–6th rounds: 1dc into each dc.

Fasten off.

x2

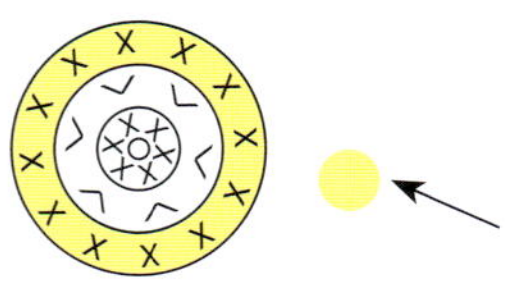

Hands (make 2)

Using yellow yarn, make a magic ring as for the head.

1st round: [3htr into next dc, 1dc into foll dc], twice, 3htr into next st.

Fasten off.

x2

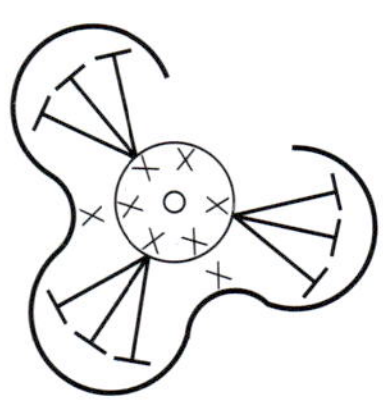

Making up

Stuff the nose, neck body, tail, legs and feet with toy stuffing. Using the photographs and the structure diagram as reference and matching yarn, stitch the nose to the head, the head to the neck, the neck to the body and the body to the tail. Stitch the feet to the legs and the legs to the body. Using green yarn, embroider straight stitches on to the nose.

For the ears, using green yarn, join into the right side of the head. Then, working into the head stitches, work the following in a straight line towards the top of the head; 1ch, 1htr into the st at base of ch, 2tr into next st, 1htr into foll st, sl st into next st.

Repeat on the left side of the head but start at a stitch level with the last stitch of the first ear and work downwards.

For the spine, using yellow yarn, join into the top of the tail near the tip. Then, working into the tail, body, neck and head stitches, work the following in a straight line towards the top of the head; [4htr into the next dc, 1dc into foll dc] repeat to the top of the head.

Chapter 2

Love and Romance

Kiss Kiss Love Birds

These feathered friends have left the flock and set up home in their very own love nest. When Love Birds find each other they bond for life so you must remember to keep this colourful couple together forever.

Size

Height: 8cm

Materials

HOOK SIZE: 3mm

YARN:

Any bright coloured yarn will work equally well

Yellow or pink for head

Blue or lilac for the body and wings

Green or blue for the tummy

Pink or green for the cheeks

Yellow for the beak

OTHER MATERIALS:

Toy filling

2 toy safety eyes, 4mm

Structure

The Love Birds are made in two sections; with wings and breast piece attached.

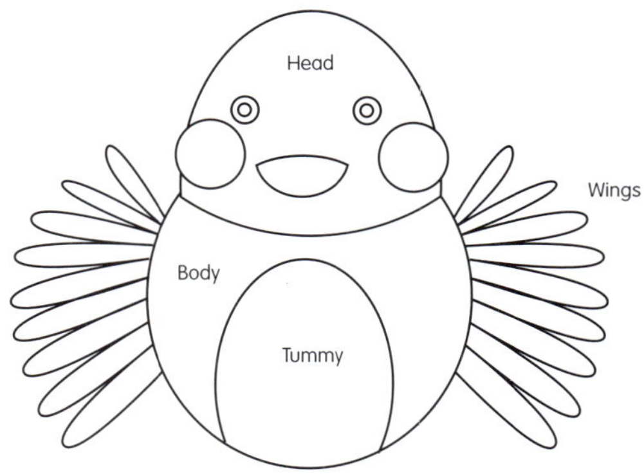

Head

Using yellow or pink yarn, make a magic ring as follows.

Make a loop with tail end of yarn on right, keeping ball end on left. Pull the ball end through loop. Make one chain through loop on hook you have drawn through to steady the circle. Work 6dc into

the circle and complete with sl st into the first dc. See also page 13.

1st round: 2dc into each dc. (12sts)

2nd round: [1dc into next dc, 2dc into foll 1dc] 6 times. (18sts)

3rd round: [1dc into each of next 2dc, 2dc into foll 1dc] 6 times. (24sts)

4th–8th rounds: 1dc into each dc.

Fasten off.

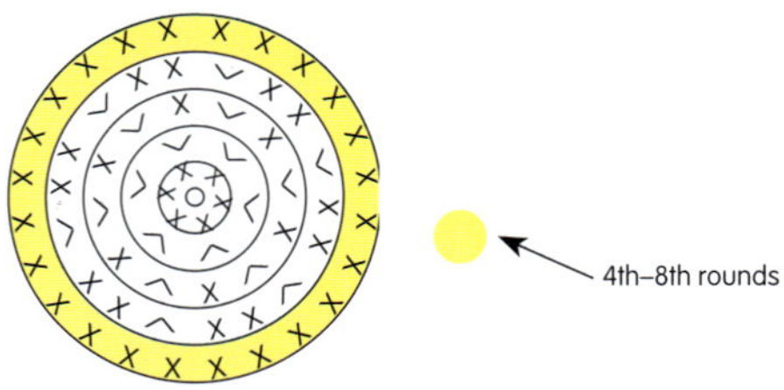

Body

Using blue or lilac yarn, make a magic ring as for the head.

1st round: 2dc into each dc. (12sts)

2nd round: [1dc into next dc, 2dc into foll dc] 6 times. (18sts)

3rd round: [1dc into each of next 2dc, 2dc into foll dc] 6 times. (24sts)

4th–7th rounds: 1dc into each dc.

8th round: [1dc into each of next 3dc, 2dc into foll dc] 6 times. (30sts)

9th round: 1dc into each dc.

10th round: [1dc into each of next 3dc, dc2tog] 6 times. (24sts)

11th round: [1dc into each of next 2dc, dc2tog] 6 times. (18sts)

12th–14th rounds: 1dc into each dc.

Fasten off.

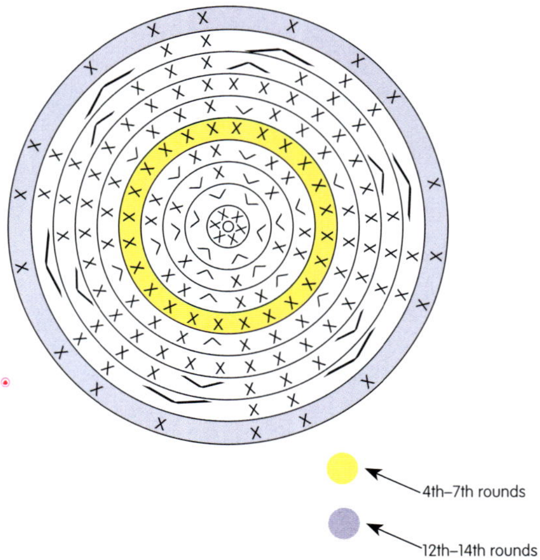

Tummy

Using green or blue yarn, make a magic ring as for the head.

1st round: 2dc into each dc. (12sts)

2nd round: [1dc into next dc, 2dc into foll dc] 6 times. (18sts)

3rd round: [1dc into each of next 2dc, 2dc into foll dc] 6 times. (24sts)

4th round: [1dc into each of next 3dc, 2dc into foll dc] 6 times. (30sts)

Fasten off.

Cheeks (make 2)

Using pink or green yarn, make a magic ring as for the head.

1st round: 2dc into each dc. (12sts)

Fasten off.

x2

Beak

Using yellow yarn, make a magic ring as for the head.

1st round: 2dc into each dc. (12sts)

2nd round: 1dc into each dc.

Fasten off.

Wings (make 2)

Work each dc with long fur stitch loops worked as follows.

Insert the hook into the place or stitch directed, hook both sets of strands hanging down on either side of the raised index finger to create a loop, draw all the strands through the fabric, remove the index finger from the loop but hold the loop firmly against the fabric, wrap the yarn around the hook and draw it through all the loops on the hook. Firmly pull on the loop to draw it tight.

Using blue or lilac yarn, make a magic ring as for the head.

1st round: 2dc into each dc. (12sts)

2nd round: [1dc into next dc, 2dc into foll dc] 6 times. (18sts)

3rd round: [1dc into each of next 2dc, 2dc into foll dc] 6 times. (24sts)

4th round: [1dc into each of next 3dc, 2dc into foll dc] 6 times. (30sts)

Fasten off.

x2

Making up

Secure the toy safety eyes approximately 4sts apart on the sixth round and stuff the head with toy filling. Using the photographs as reference and matching yarn, stitch the beak and cheek pieces to the head. Stuff the body with toy filling and stitch the head, tummy and wings in place. These little birds are forever!

Big Heart Bear

With his cute little face and cuddly charms, who could resist Big Heart Bear? He's on a mission to spread the love around. Make him for your special someone and their heart will be yours forever.

Size

Height: 16cm

Materials

HOOK SIZE: 3mm

YARN:

Brown for the head, body, arms, legs and ears.

Light brown for the heart tummy

Yellow for the nose

OTHER MATERIALS:

Toy filling

2 toy safety eyes, 8mm

Head

Using brown yarn, make a magic ring as follows.

Make a loop with tail end of yarn on right, keeping ball end on left. Pull the ball end through loop. Make one chain through loop on hook you have drawn through to steady the circle. Work 6dc into the circle and complete with sl st into the first dc. See also page 13.

1st round: 2dc into each dc. (12sts)

2nd round: [1dc into next dc, 2dc into foll 1dc] 6 times. (18sts)

3rd round: [1dc into each of next 2dc, 2dc into foll 1dc] 6 times. (24sts)

4th round: [1dc into each of next 3dc, 2dc into foll dc] 6 times. (30sts)

5th round: [1dc into each of next 4dc, 2dc into foll dc] 6 times. (36sts)

6th round: [1dc into each of next 5dc, 2dc into foll dc] 6 times. (42sts)

7th–9th rounds: 1dc into each dc.

10th round: [1dc into each of next 5dc, dc2tog] 6 times. (36sts)

11th round: [1dc into each of next 4dc, dc2tog] 6 times. (30sts)

12th round: [1dc into each of next 3dc, dc2tog] 6 times. (24sts)

13th round: [1dc into each of next 2dc, dc2tog] 6 times. (18sts)

Secure the toy safety eyes approximately 7sts apart on the seventh round and stuff the head with toy filling.

14th round: [1dc into next dc, dc2tog] 6 times. (12sts)

15th round: [dc2tog] 6 times. (6sts)

Fasten off.

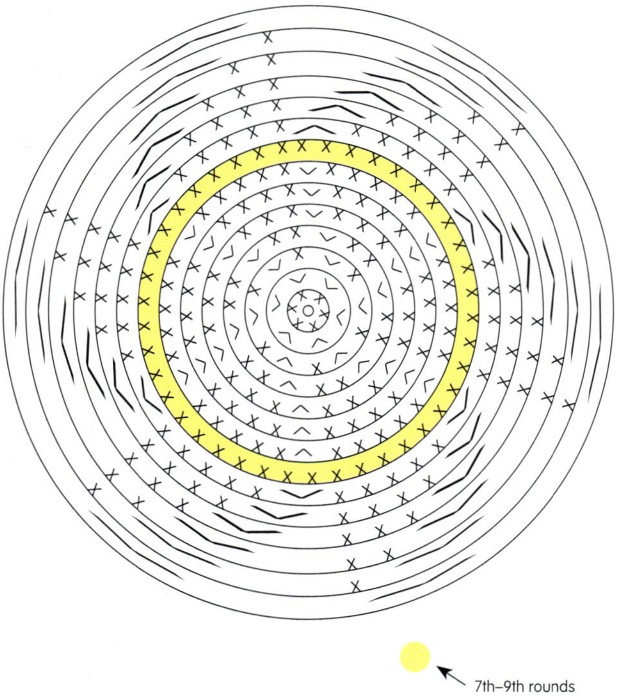

Body

Using brown yarn, make a magic ring as for the head.

1st round: 2dc into each dc. (12sts)

2nd round: [1dc into next dc, 2dc into foll dc] 6 times. (18sts)

3rd round: [1dc into each of next 2dc, 2dc into foll dc] 6 times. (24sts)

4th–7th rounds: 1dc into each dc.

8th round: [1dc into each of next 2dc, dc2tog] 6 times. (18sts)

9th–10th rounds: 1dc into each dc.

11th round: [1dc into next dc, dc2tog] 6 times. (12sts)

12th–13th rounds: 1dc into each dc.

Fasten off.

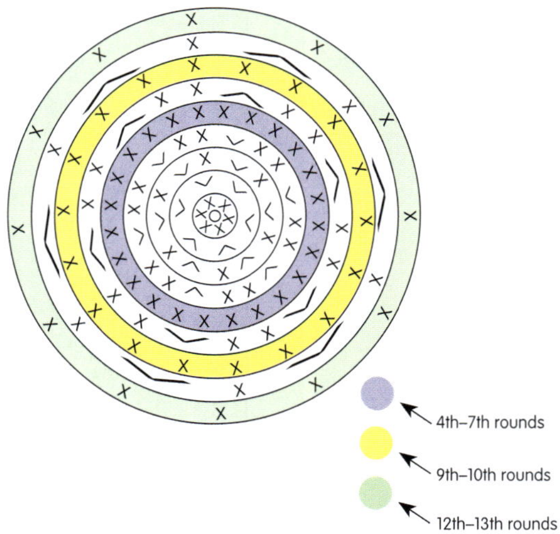

Arms (make 2)

Using brown yarn, make a magic ring as for the head.

1st round: 2dc into each dc. (12sts)

2nd–12th rounds: 1dc into each dc.

Fasten off.

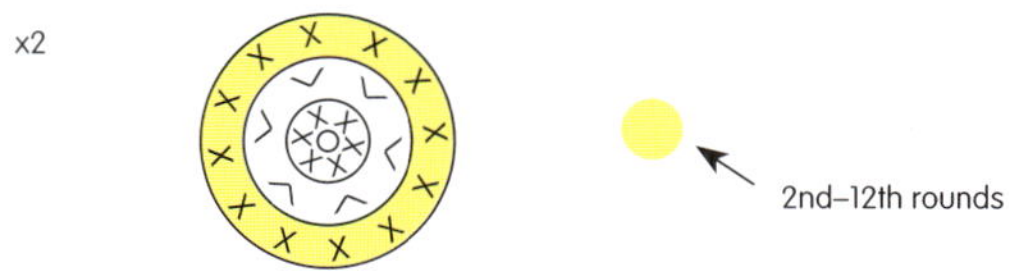

Legs (make 2)

Using brown yarn, make a magic ring as for the head.

Work as for Legs until 9th round.

Fasten off.

Ears (make 2)

Using brown yarn, make a magic ring as for the head.

Work as for Legs until 4th round.

Fasten off.

Nose

Using yellow yarn, make a magic ring as for the head.

Work as for Legs until 4th round.

Fasten off.

Heart tummy

Using light brown yarn, make a magic ring as for the head.

1st round: 2dc into each dc. (12sts)

2nd round: 1dc into each dc

3rd round: 1ch, 1dc into next dc, 3htr into foll 1dc, 1dc into each of next 2dc, 3htr into next dc, 1dc into foll dc, sl st into the next 2dc, 1dc into each of the next 2dc, sl st into next 2dc.

Fasten off.

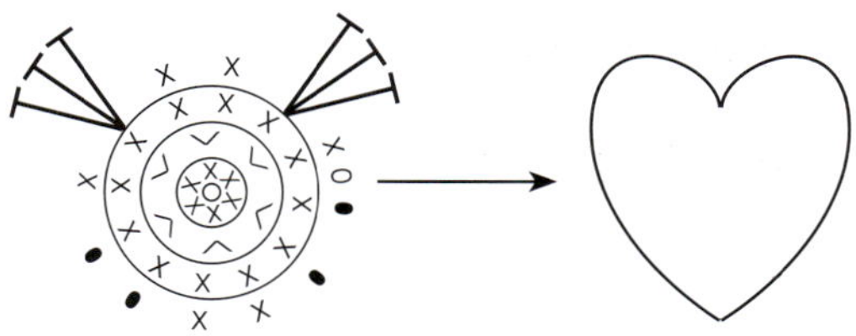

Making up

Using the photographs as reference and matching yarn, stitch the flattened ears and nose to the head.

Stuff the body, arms and legs with toy filling. Stitch the head, heart tummy, arms and legs to the body. Time for the heart bear's first hug!

Wedding Joy

When the happy couple seal the knot, then it's time to get out the yarn and make this blushing bride and groom for their very own woolly wedding. Create this crocheted Mr. and Mrs. and celebrate matrimonial bliss.

Size

Bride's height: 14cm

Materials

HOOK SIZE: 3mm

YARN:

Flesh-coloured for both heads and noses

Red for the cheeks

Brown for the bride's hair

White for the dress and two bows.

Grey for the top hat and groom's suit

OTHER MATERIALS:

Toy filling

4 toy safety eyes, 8mm

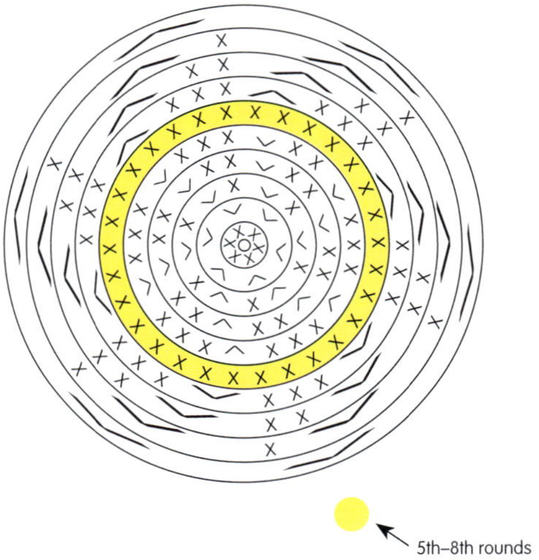

Bride's head

Using flesh-coloured yarn, make a magic ring as follows.

Make a loop with tail end of yarn on right, keeping ball end on left. Pull the ball end through loop. Make one chain through loop on hook you have drawn through to steady the circle. Work 6dc into the circle and complete with sl st into the first dc. See also page 13.

1st round: 2dc into each dc. (12sts)

2nd round: [1dc into next dc, 2dc into foll 1dc] 6 times. (18sts)

Ciro

3rd round: [1dc into each of next 2dc, 2dc into foll 1dc] 6 times. (24sts)

4th round: [1dc into each of next 3dc, 2dc into foll dc] 6 times. (30sts)

5th–8th rounds: 1dc into each dc.

9th round: [1dc into each of next 3dc, dc2tog] 6 times. (24sts)

10th round: [1dc into each of next 2dc, dc2tog] 6 times. (18sts)

Secure the toy safety eyes approximately 6sts apart on the sixth round and stuff the head with toy filling.

11th round: [1dc into next dc, dc2tog] 6 times. (12sts)

12th round: [dc2tog] 6 times. (6sts)

Fasten off.

Bride's cheeks (make 2)

Using red yarn, make a magic ring as for the bride's head.

Fasten off.

x2

Bride's nose

Using flesh-coloured yarn, make a magic ring as for the bride's head.

1st–2nd rounds: 1dc into each dc.

Fasten off.

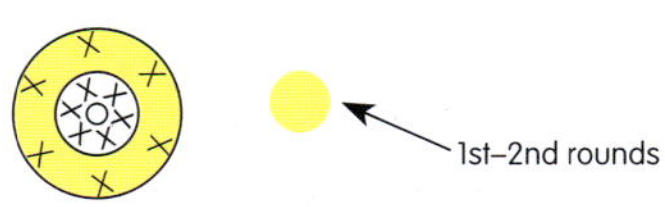

Bride's hair

4tr-bobble = [wrap the yarn around the hook, insert the hook into fourth ch from hook, wrap yarn around hook, draw yarn through ch, wrap yarn around hook draw yarn through two loops on hook] 4 times, wrap yarn around hook draw yarn through all loops on the hook.

Using brown yarn, make 4ch

1st row: 4tr-bobble [4ch, 4tr-bobble] 27 times or as many times as you wish to curl around the bride's head.

Fasten off.

x2

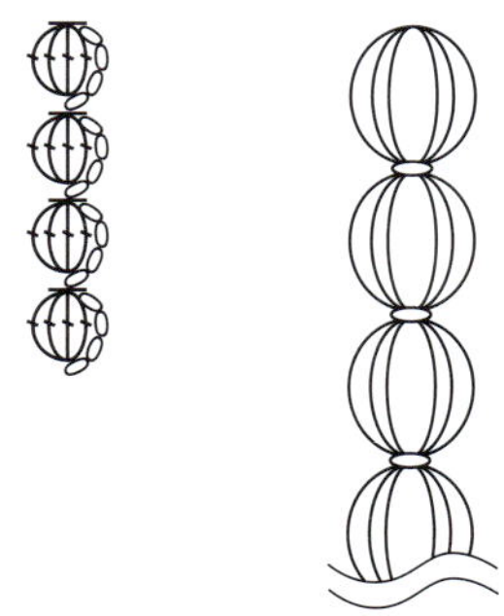

Bride's dress

Using white yarn, make a magic ring as for the bride's head.

1st round: 2dc into each dc. (12sts)

2nd round: [1dc into next dc, 2dc into foll dc] 6 times. (18sts)

3rd round: [1dc into each of next 2dc, 2dc into foll dc] 6 times. (24sts)

4th–18th rounds: 1dc into each dc.

Fasten off.

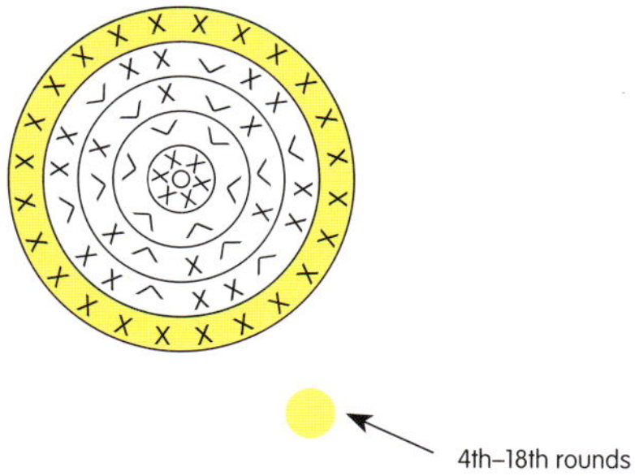

Bride's dress base

Using white yarn, make a magic ring as for the bride's head.

Work as for Bride's dress until 3rd round.

Fasten off.

Bride's bow

Using white, make 15ch.

1st row: 1htr into the third ch from the hook, 1htr into each ch to end, turn. (14sts)

2nd–4th rows: 2ch (counts as first htr), 1htr into the back loop of each htr to end, turn.

Fasten off white yarn, join in cream.

5th–8th rows: 2ch (counts as first htr), 1htr into the back loop of each htr to end, turn.

Fasten off.

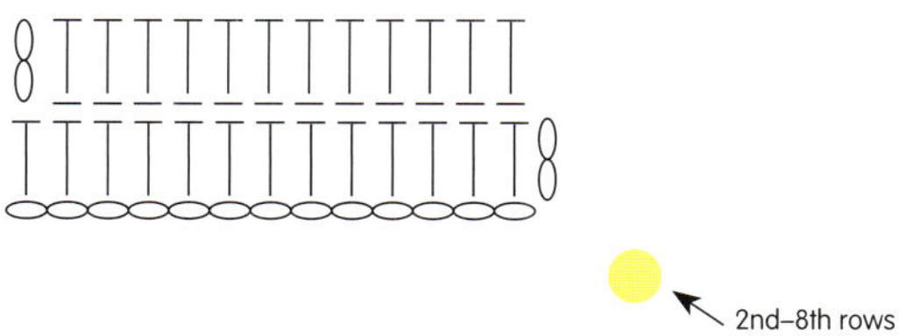

Groom's head

Using flesh-coloured yarn, make a magic ring as for the bride's head.

Work as for bride's head.

Groom's cheeks (make 2)

Using red yarn, make a magic ring as for the bride's head.

Work as for bride's cheeks.

Groom's nose

Using flesh-coloured yarn, make a magic ring as for the bride's head.

Work as for groom's cheeks.

Groom's suit body

Using grey yarn, make a magic ring as for the bride's head.

1st round: 2dc into each dc. (12sts)

2nd round: [1dc into next dc, 2dc into foll dc] 6 times. (18sts)

3rd round: [1dc into each of next 2dc, 2dc into foll dc] 6 times. (24sts)

4th round: [1dc into each of next 3dc, 2dc into foll dc] 6 times. (30sts)

5th–7th rounds: 1dc into each dc.

8th round: [1dc into each of next 3dc, dc2tog] 6 times. (24sts)

9th–10th rounds: 1dc into each dc.

11th round: [1dc into each of next 2dc, dc2tog] 6 times. (18sts)

12th–14th rounds: 1dc into each dc.

Fasten off.

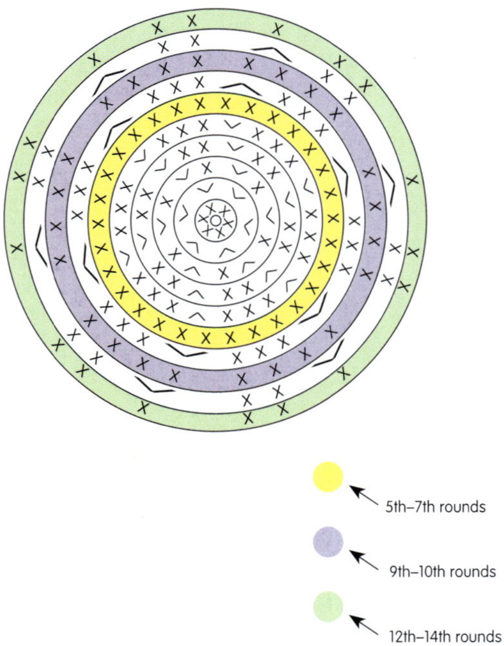

Groom's legs (make 2)

Using grey yarn, make a magic ring as for the bride's head.

1st round: 2dc into each dc. (12sts)

2nd round: [1dc into next dc, 2dc into foll dc] 6 times. (18sts)

3rd–9th rounds: 1dc into each dc.

Fasten off.

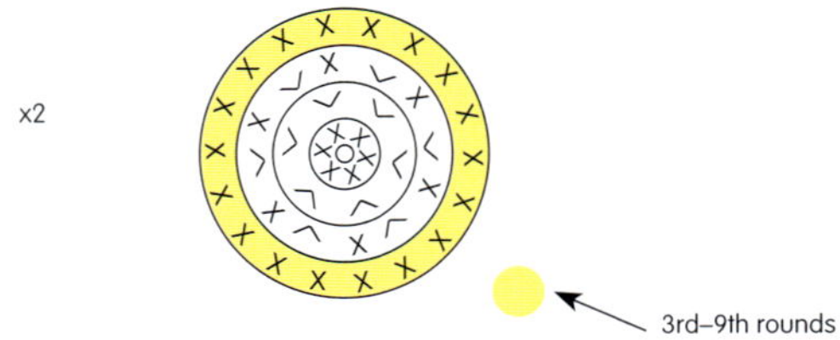

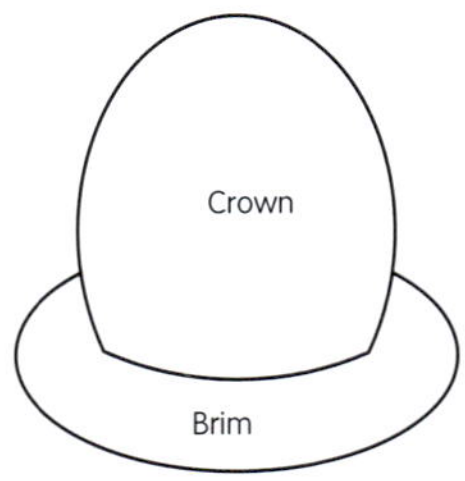

Groom's hat crown

Using grey yarn, make a magic ring as for the bride's head.

1st round: 2dc into each dc. (12sts)

2nd–6th rounds: 1dc into each dc.

Fasten off.

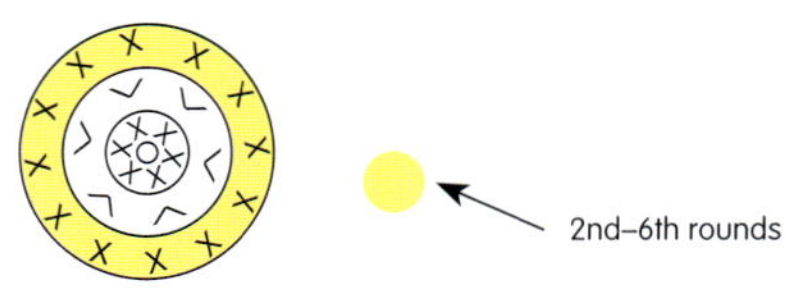

Groom's hat brim

Using grey yarn, make a magic ring as for the bride's head.

1st round: 2dc into each dc. (12sts)

2nd round: [1dc into next dc, 2dc into foll dc] 6 times. (18sts)

3rd round: [1dc into each of next 2dc, 2dc into foll dc] 6 times. (24sts)

Fasten off.

Groom's bow tie

Using white, make 8ch.

1st row: 1htr into the third ch from the hook, 1htr into each ch to end, turn. (6sts)

2nd–4th rows: 2ch (counts as first htr), 1htr into each dc to end, turn.

Fasten off.

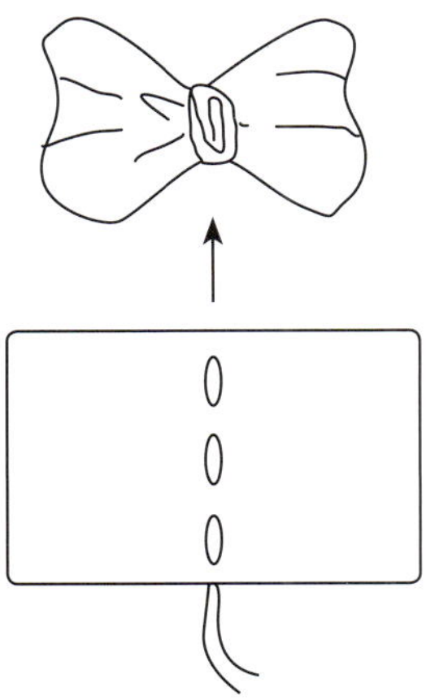

Making up

Using the photographs as reference and matching yarn, stitch the cheeks and nose to the bride's head. Starting from the centre, wrap and pin the bride's hair around her head in a spiral, until it reaches ear level, then work back and forth, from side to side, in an S-shape. Stitch in place. Repeat for the groom but skip the hair instructions and instead, stuff the hat crown, stitch it to the hat brim and stitch both on to the groom's head.

To finish the bows; fold the bride's bow in half horizontally and stitch the top and bottom edges together; fold the groom's bow in half lengthways and stitch the selvedge edges together. Using white or cream yarn, stitch a line of running stitches around the centre of the tube, pull tight and secure, wrap yarn tightly around the centre of the bow and secure.

Stuff the dress with toy filling. Attach the bride's head and the bride's bow to the dress.

Stuff the suit body and legs with toy filling. Attach the groom's head and legs to the suit body. Using black yarn, embroider, lapel outlines onto the groom's suit. Attach the groom's bow tie to the suit.

Red Red Rose

The age of romance is not dead! If you're totally smitten there's nothing like a single, red rose when you want to make an amourous gesture. Surprise your loved one with a tender token that will last forever.

Size

Height: 17cm

Materials

HOOK SIZE: 3mm

YARN:

Red for the rose head

Green for the leaf and stem

OTHER MATERIALS:

Craft wire, 15cm

Rose head

Using red yarn, make 36ch or a ch longer than 20cm for a rose head size of your choice!

1st row: 2tr into the fourth ch from the hook, 2tr into each ch to end.

Fasten off.

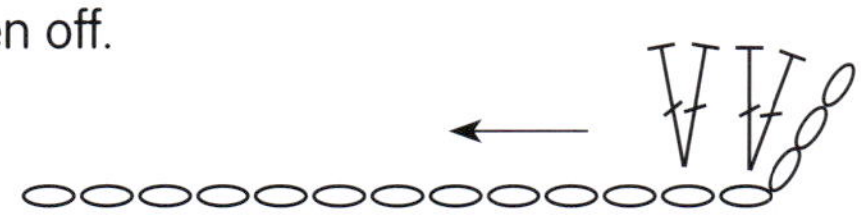

Stem

Using green yarn, make a ch the same length as the craft wire.

Holding the wire and the chain together in the left hand (for right-handed crocheters), work the following row around the wire and encase the craft wire with double crochet stitches.

1st row: 1dc into the second ch from the hook, 1dc into each ch to end.

Fasten off.

Leaf

Using green yarn, make 9ch.

1st row: 1dc into the third ch from the hook, 1htr into next ch, 1tr into each of next 2ch, 1htr into foll ch, 1dc into each of last 2ch.

Fasten off.

Making up

Using the photographs as reference and matching yarn, roll the rose head up along its length and secure at the base with a few stitches. Stitch the leaf to the stem and the stem to the underside of the rose head.

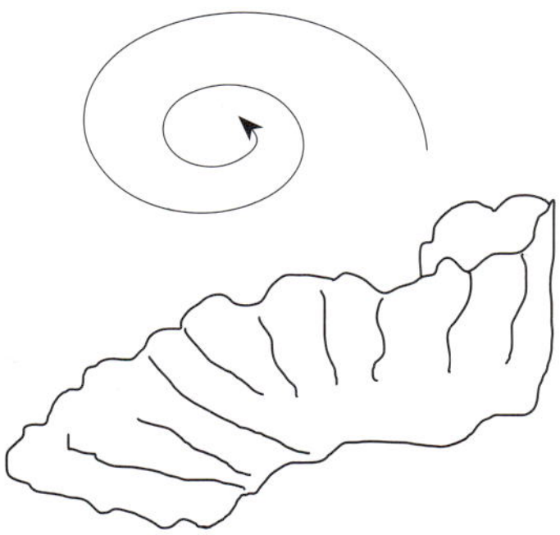

Chapter 3

Springtime is Here!

Springtime Ducks

When cute little baby animals start to appear, it's a sure sign that spring has arrived. So when winter's over and the days start to warm up, it's time to get quacking and create your own darling duckling.

Size

Height with top tuft: 10cm

Materials

HOOK SIZE: 3mm

YARN:

Dark yellow for the head, body and wings

Orange for beak

OTHER MATERIALS:

Toy filling

2 toy safety eyes, 8mm

Structure

The Easter chick is made in two sections; with wings and a hair tuft attached.

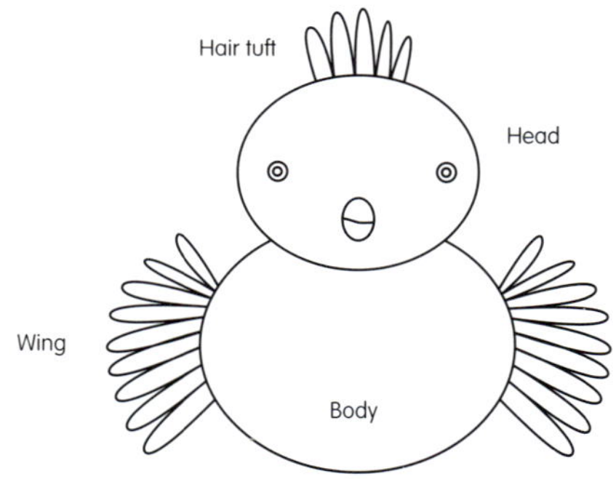

Head

Using dark yellow yarn, make a magic ring as follows.

Make a loop with tail end of yarn on right, keeping ball end on left. Pull the ball end through loop. Make one chain through loop on hook you have drawn through to steady the circle. Work 6dc into the circle and complete with sl st into the first dc. See also page 13.

1st round: 2dc into each dc. (12sts)

2nd round: [1dc into next dc, 2dc into foll 1dc] 6 times. (18sts)

3rd round: [1dc into each of next 2dc, 2dc into foll 1dc] 6 times. (24sts)

4th–8th rounds: 1dc into each dc.

9th round: [1dc into each of next 2dc, dc2tog] 6 times. (18sts)

Secure the toy safety eyes approximately 8sts apart on the seventh round and stuff with toy filling.

11th round: [1dc into next dc, dc2tog] 6 times. (12sts)

12th round: [dc2tog] 6 times. (6sts)

Fasten off.

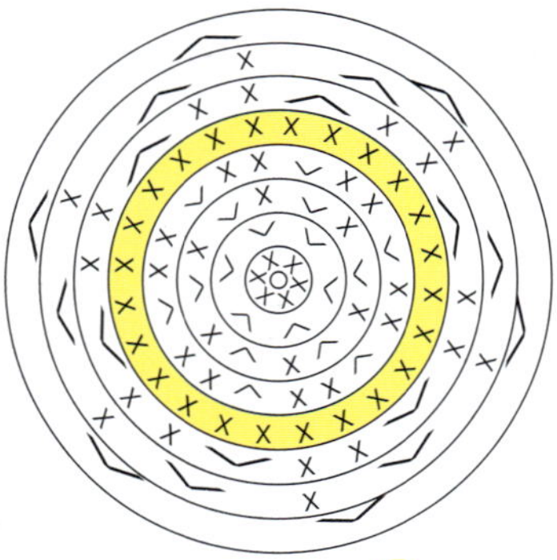

Body

Using dark yellow yarn, make a magic ring as for the head.

1st round: 2dc into each dc. (12sts)

2nd round: [1dc into next dc, 2dc into foll dc] 6 times. (18sts)

3rd round: [1dc into each of next 2dc, 2dc into foll dc] 6 times. (24sts)

4th round: [1dc into each of next 3dc, 2dc into foll dc] 6 times. (30sts)

5th round: [1dc into each of next 4dc, 2dc into foll dc] 6 times. (36sts)

6th round: [1dc into each of next 5dc, 2dc into foll dc] 6 times. (42sts)

7th–12th rounds: 1dc into each dc

13th round: [1dc into each of next 5dc, dc2tog] 6 times. (36sts)

14th round: [1dc into each of next 4dc, dc2tog] 6 times. (30sts)

15th round: [1dc into each of next 3dc, dc2tog] 6 times. (24sts)

16th round: [1dc into each of next 2dc, dc2tog] 6 times. (18sts)

17th round: [1dc into next dc, dc2tog] 6 times. (12sts)

18th round: [dc2tog] 6 times. (6sts)

Fasten off.

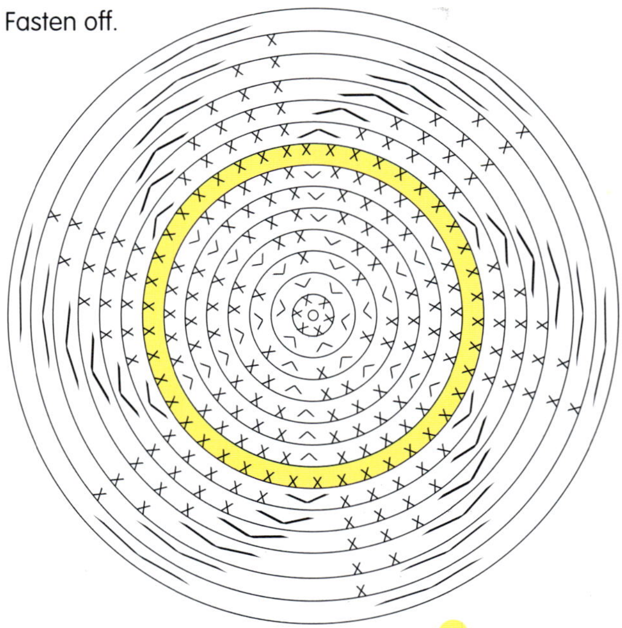

Beak (make 2)

Using orange yarn, make 5ch.

1st row: 1dc into the second ch from the hook, 1dc into each ch to end, turn. (4sts)

2nd row: 1ch (counts as first dc), 1dc into each dc to end, turn.

3rd row: 1ch (counts as first dc), dc2tog, 1dc into last dc, turn.

4th row: 1ch (counts as first dc), dc2tog.

Fasten off.

x2

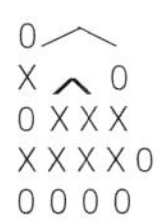

Wings (make 2)

Work each dc with long fur stitch loops worked as follows.

Insert the hook into the place or stitch directed, hook both sets of strands hanging down either side of the raised index finger to create a loop, draw all the strands through the fabric, remove the index finger from the loop but hold the loop firmly against the fabric, wrap the yarn around the hook and draw it through all the loops on the hook. Firmly pull on the loop to draw it tight.

Using double stranded dark yellow yarn, make a magic ring as for the head.

1st round: 2dc into each dc. (12sts)

2nd round: [1dc into next dc, 2dc into foll dc] 6 times. (18sts)

3rd round: [1dc into each of next 2dc, 2dc into foll dc] 6 times. (24sts)

4th round: [1dc into each of next 3dc, 2dc into foll dc] 6 times. (30sts)

Fasten off.

x2

Hair tuft

Work each dc with long fur stitch loops worked as above for the wings.

Using double stranded dark yellow yarn, make a magic ring as for the head.

1st round: 2dc into each dc. (12sts)

Fasten off.

x2

Making up

Using the photographs as reference and matching yarn, stitch the beak pieces to the face and the hair tuft to the head.

Stuff the body with toy filling. To create the flattened shape of the body, secure a length of yarn to the centre of the base, stitch through the depth of the body, pull tight and secure the shape with a stitch. Stitch the head and wings to the body. Isn't it tweet?

Dancing Daffodils

You know that spring has well and truly sprung when beautiful blooms start bursting out all over. Sunshine yellow and full of joy, these dancing daffodils are set to brighten up any day.

Size

Height: 17cm

Materials

HOOK SIZE: 3mm

YARN:

Cream or yellow for the petals

Yellow or orange for the flower centre

Green for the stem

OTHER MATERIALS:

Craft wire, 15cm

Petal (make 6)

Using cream or yellow yarn, make 7ch.

1st row: 1dc into the second ch from the hook, 1dc into each ch to end. (6sts)

2nd–3rd rows: 1ch, 1dc into each dc to end.

4th row: 1ch, 1dc into next dc, [dc2tog] twice, 1dc into next dc. (4sts)

5th row: 1ch, 1dc into each dc to end.

6th row: 1ch, 1dc into next dc, dc2tog, 1dc into next dc. (3sts)

7th row: 1ch, dc2tog.

Fasten off

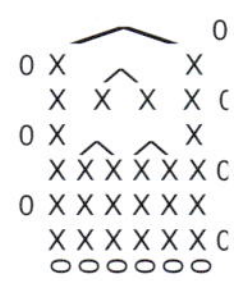

x6

Flower centre

Using yellow or orange yarn, make a magic ring as follows.

Make a loop with tail end of yarn on right, keeping ball end on left. Pull the ball end through loop. Make one chain through loop on hook you have drawn through to steady the circle. Work 6dc into the circle and complete with sl st into the first dc. See also page 13.

1st round: 2dc into each dc. (12sts)

2nd–5th rounds: 1dc into each dc.

Fasten off.

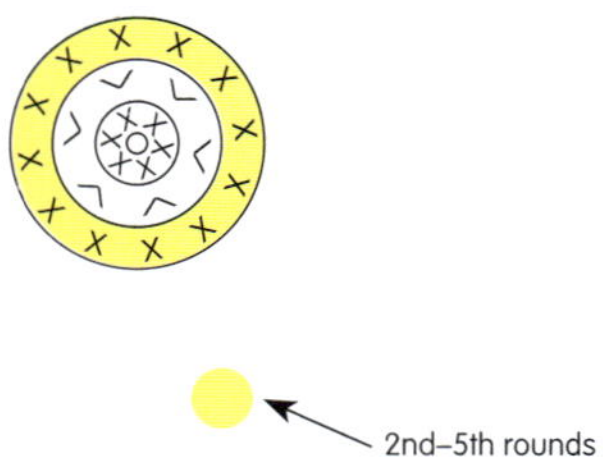

Stem

Using green yarn, make a magic ring as for the flower centre.

Work 1dc into each dc until the piece measures 15cm.

Fasten off.

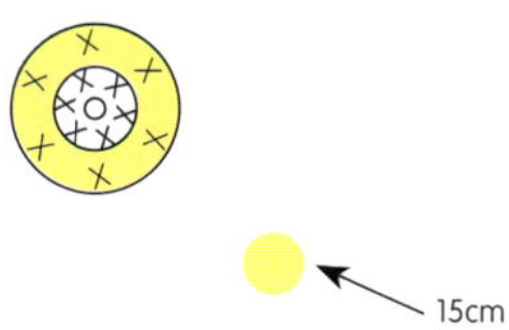

Making up

Using the photographs as reference and matching yarn, stitch the flower petals to the flower centre. Make a small loop at either end of the craft wire, slide the craft wire into the centre of the stem and stitch through the wire loops to secure it in place. Stitch the stem to the underside of the flower head.

You have just made it!

Eggs in Basket

If you want a really egg-citing gift for an eggs-tra special friend, then why not make them happy with a jolly striped egg? Make half a dozen of them and you can put all your eggs in one basket whenever you want.

Size

Length: 6cm

Materials

Green 4

HOOK SIZE: 3mm

YARN:

Any yarn or colour

OTHER MATERIALS:

Toy filling

Using yarn of your choice, make a magic ring as follows.

Make a loop with tail end of yarn on right, keeping ball end on left. Pull the ball end through loop. Make one chain through loop on hook you have drawn through to steady the circle. Work 6dc into the circle and complete with sl st into the first dc. See also page 13.

1st round: 2dc into each dc. (12sts)

2nd round: [1dc into next dc, 2dc into foll 1dc] 6 times. (18sts)

3rd round: [1dc into each of next 2dc, 2dc into foll 1dc] 6 times. (24sts)

4th–11th rounds: 1dc into each dc.

12th round: [1dc into each of next 2dc, dc2tog] 6 times. (18sts)

Stuff the egg with toy filling.

13th round: [1dc into next dc, dc2tog] 6 times. (12sts)

14th round: [dc2tog] 6 times. (6sts)

Fasten off.

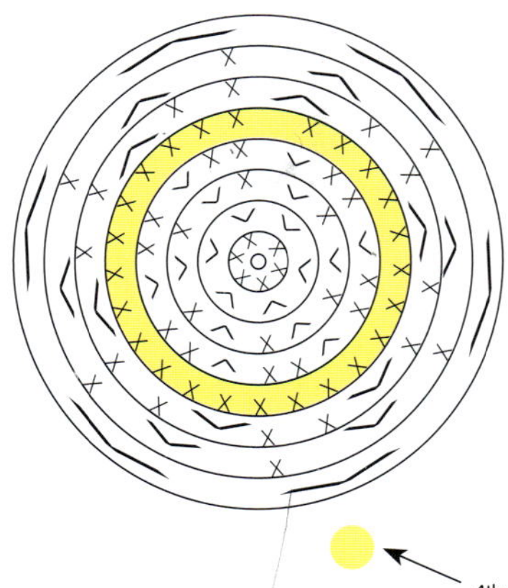

4th–11th rounds

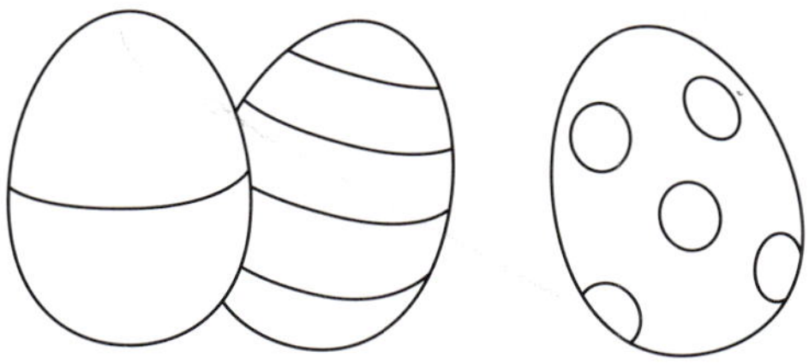

Using different yarns and embroidery stitches design your own eggs and then have fun, hiding them for others to find!

Hop Hop Easter Bunny!

At Easter time this bouncy bunny is bound to bring a super-sweet surprise or two, but you have to find them first! If you give him a big cuddle, maybe he'll tell you where all the chocolate is hidden.

Size

Height: 17cm

Materials

HOOK SIZE: 3mm

YARN:

White for the head, body, arms, legs, feet, tail, ears and nose

Pink for the cheeks

Brown for the embroider of the mouth

OTHER MATERIALS:

Toy filling

2 black beads, 4mm

Head

Using white yarn, make a magic ring as follows.

Make a loop with tail end of yarn on right, keeping ball end on left. Pull the ball end through loop. Make one chain through loop on hook you have drawn through to steady the circle. Work 6dc into the circle and complete with sl st into the first dc. See also page 13.

1st round: 2dc into each dc. (12sts)

2nd round: [1dc into next dc, 2dc into foll 1dc] 6 times. (18sts)

3rd round: [1dc into each of next 2dc, 2dc into foll 1dc] 6 times. (24sts)

4th round: [1dc into each of next 3dc, 2dc into foll 1dc] 6 times. (30sts)

5th–10th rounds: 1dc into each dc.

11th round: [1dc into each of next 3dc, dc2tog] 6 times. (24sts)

12th round: [1dc into each of next 2dc, dc2tog] 6 times. (18sts)

Secure the toy safety eyes approximately 6sts apart on the eighth round and stuff with toy filling.

13th round: [1dc into next dc, dc2tog] 6 times. (12sts)

14th round: [dc2tog] 6 times. (6sts)

Fasten off.

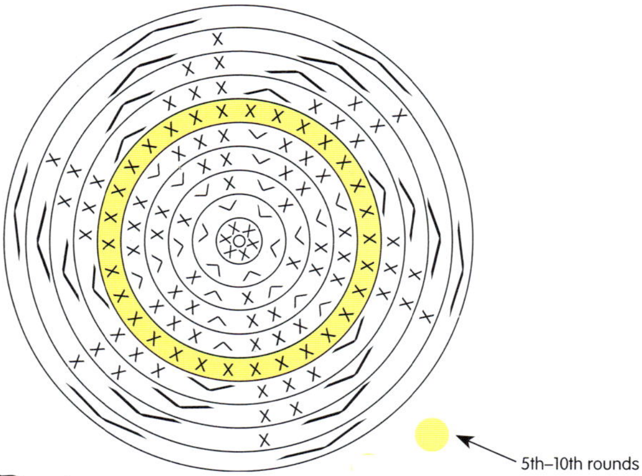

Body

Using white yarn, make a magic ring as for the head.

1st round: 2dc into each dc. (12sts)

2nd round: [1dc into next dc, 2dc into foll dc] 6 times. (18sts)

3rd round: [1dc into each of next 2dc, 2dc into foll dc] 6 times. (24sts)

4th round: [1dc into each of next 3dc, 2dc into foll dc] 6 times. (30sts)

5th–10th rounds: 1dc into each dc.

11th round: [1dc into each of next 3dc, dc2tog] 6 times. (24sts)

12th round: [1dc into each of next 2dc, dc2tog] 6 times. (18sts)

13th–14th rounds: 1dc into each dc.

Stuff the body with toy filling.

15th round: [1dc into next dc, dc2tog] 6 times. (12sts)

16th–17th rounds: 1dc into each dc.

Fasten off.

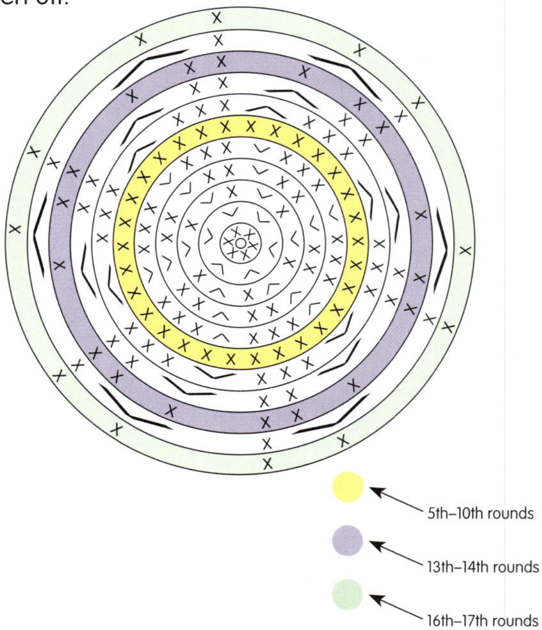

Cheeks (make 2)

Using pink yarn, make a magic ring as for the head.

1st round: 2dc into each dc. (12sts)

2nd–3rd rounds: 1dc into each dc.

Fasten off.

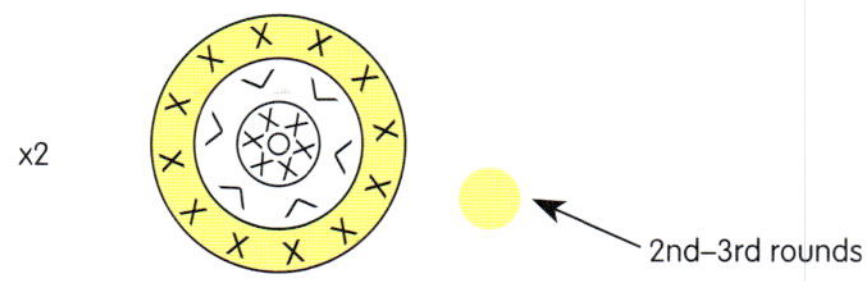

Nose and Tail

Using white yarn, make a magic ring as for the head.

Work one piece for each as for cheeks.

Ears (make 2)

Using white yarn, make a magic ring as for the head.

1st round: 2dc into each dc. (12sts)

2nd–12th rounds: 1dc into each dc.

Fasten off.

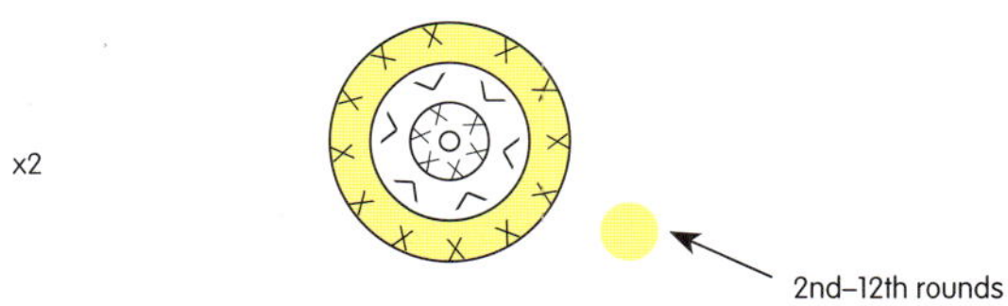

Legs (make 2)

Using white yarn, make a magic ring as for the head.

1st round: 2dc into each dc. (12sts)

2nd round: [1dc into next dc, 2dc into foll dc] 6 times. (18sts)

3rd-6th rounds: 1dc into each dc.

Fasten off.

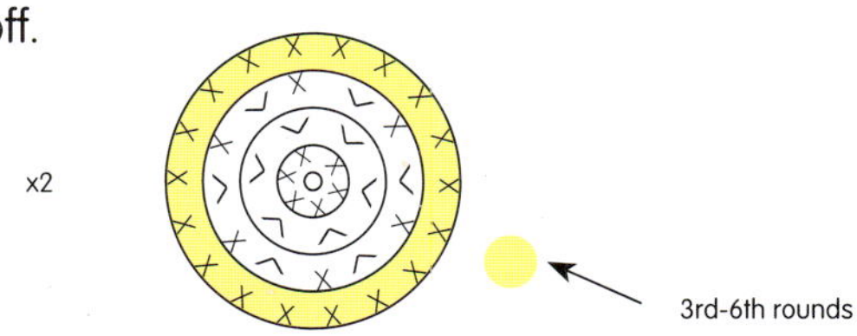

Feet (make 2)

Using white yarn, make a magic ring as for the head.

1st round: 2dc into each dc. (12sts)

2nd–4th rounds: 1dc into each dc.

Fasten off.

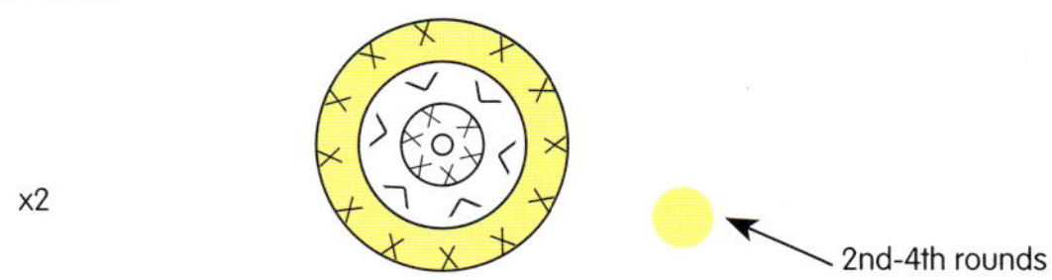

Arms (make 2)

Using white yarn, make a magic ring as for the head.

1st round: 2dc into each dc. (12sts)

2nd–6th rounds: 1dc into each dc.

Fasten off.

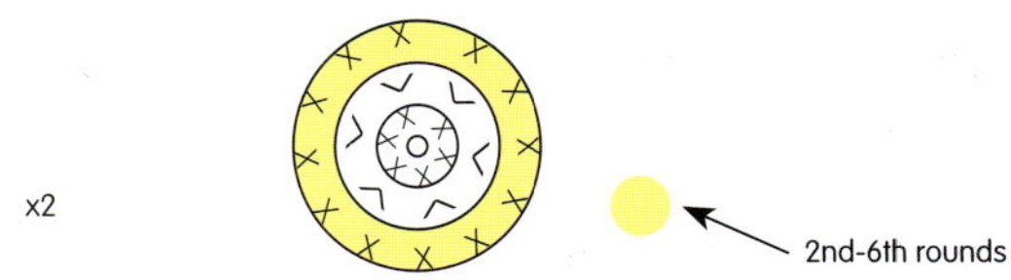

Making up

Using the photographs as reference and matching yarn, stitch the flattened ears, cheeks and nose to the head. Using brown yarn, embroider the nose.

Stuff the body and legs with toy filling. Do not stuff the arms and feet. Stitch the head to the body, the arms on the front of the body and the legs to the side of the body. Stitch the feet to the legs and the tail to the back of the body. With a twitch of the nose, your bunny is ready to hop off!

Chapter 4

Party Time!

Party Animal

When you're planning the perfect party, don't forget an invite for this perky little panda. There's nothing he likes more than a good shindig, so make sure he's on the guest list if you want things to go with a bang.

Size

Height: 16cm

Materials

HOOK SIZE: 3mm

YARN:

White for the head and nose

Brown for the ears, eye patches, nose, arms and legs

Pink for the hat

Bright green for the hat decoration

OTHER MATERIALS:

Toy filling

2 toy safety eyes, 8mm

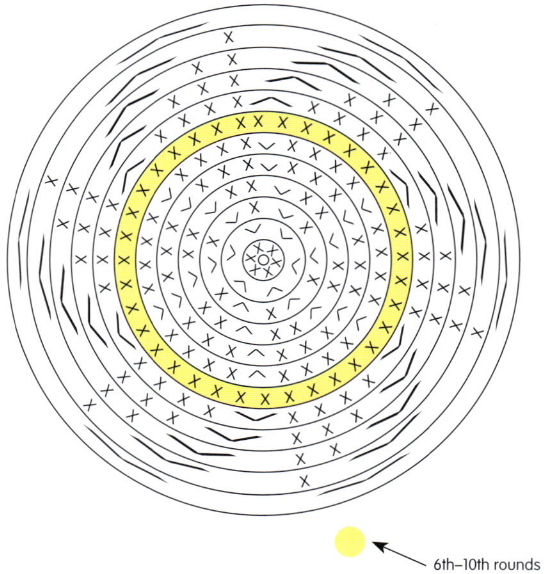

Head

Using brown yarn, make a magic ring as follows.

Make a loop with tail end of yarn on right, keeping ball end on left. Pull the ball end through loop. Make one chain through loop on hook you have drawn through to steady the circle. Work 6dc into the circle and complete with sl st into the first dc. See also page 13.

1st round: 2dc into each dc. (12sts)

2nd round: [1dc into next dc, 2dc into foll 1dc] 6 times. (18sts)

3rd round: [1dc into each of next 2dc, 2dc into foll 1dc] 6 times. (24sts)

4th round: [1dc into each of next 3dc, 2dc into foll 1dc] 6 times. (30sts)

5th round: [1dc into each of next 4dc, 2dc into foll 1dc] 6 times. (36sts)

6th–10th rounds: 1dc into each dc.

11th round: [1dc into each of next 4dc, dc2tog] 6 times. (30sts)

12th round: [1dc into each of next 3dc, dc2tog] 6 times. (24sts)

13th round: [1dc into each of next 2dc, dc2tog] 6 times. (18sts)

Stuff the head with toy filling.

14th round: [1dc into next dc, dc2tog] 6 times. (12sts)

15th round: [dc2tog] 6 times. (6sts)

Fasten off.

Body

Using white yarn, make a magic ring as for the head.

1st round: 2dc into each dc. (12sts)

2nd round: [1dc into next dc, 2dc into foll dc] 6 times. (18sts)

3rd round: [1dc into each of next 2dc, 2dc into foll dc] 6 times. (24sts)

4th–5th rounds: 1dc into each dc.

6th round: [1dc into each of next 2dc, dc2tog] 6 times. (18sts)

7th–14th rounds: 1dc into each dc.

Fasten off.

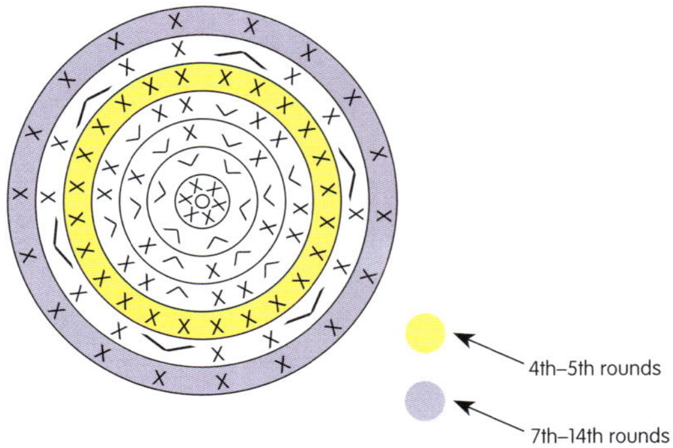

Legs (make 2)

Using brown yarn, make a magic ring as for the head.

1st round: 2dc into each dc. (12sts)

2nd–8th rounds: 1dc into each dc.

Fasten off.

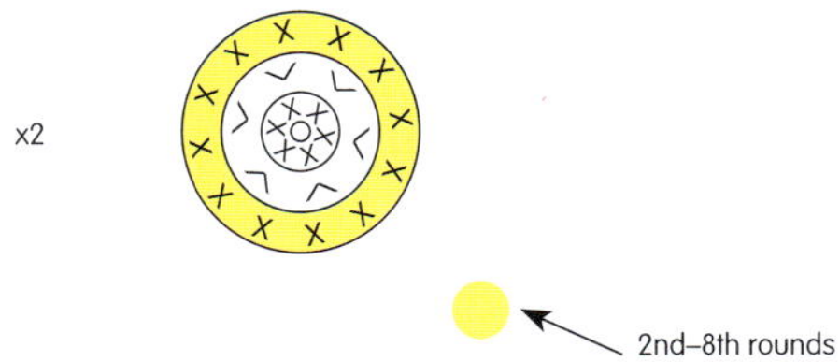

Arms (make 2)

Using brown yarn, make a magic ring as for the head.

Work as for legs.

Eye patches (make 2)

Using brown yarn, make a magic ring as for the head.

1st round: 2dc into each dc. (12sts)

Fasten off.

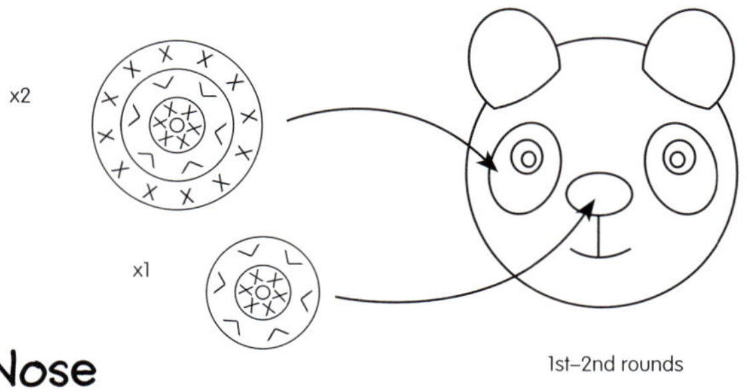

Nose

Using brown yarn, make a magic ring as for the head.

1st–2nd rounds: 1dc into each dc.

Fasten off.

Ears (make 2)

Using brown yarn, make a magic ring as for the head.

1st round: 2dc into each dc. (12sts)

2nd–4th rounds: 1dc into each dc.

Fasten off.

Hat

Using pink yarn, make a magic ring as for the head.

1st–2nd rounds: 1dc into each dc.

3rd round: 2dc into each dc. (12sts)

4th–5th rounds: 1dc into each dc.

6th round: [1dc into next dc, 2dc into foll dc] 6 times. (18sts)

7th–8th rounds: 1dc into each dc.

Fasten off.

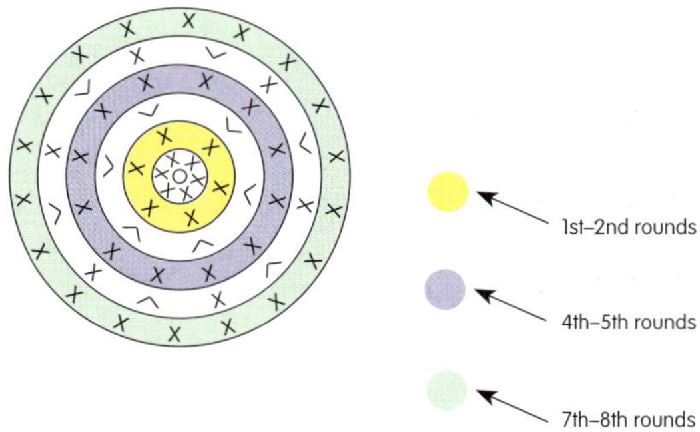

Making up

Stuff the head, body, legs, arms and hat with toy stuffing.

Attach the toy safety eyes to the eye patches.

Using the photographs as reference and matching yarn, stitch the nose, eyes and flattened ears to the head and the head to the body. Stitch the legs and arms to the body.

Using brown yarn, embroider straight stitches for the mouth. Using green yarn, embroider straight stitch blocks on to the hat. And then, at a jaunty angle, put the hat on him; joy!

Special Gifts

We all love a beautifully wrapped present so why not make the gift-wrap the gift? Make these beribboned little boxes to mark any memorable occasion and you can be certain of spreading a little happiness.

Size

Height: 7cm

Width: 7cm

Materials

HOOK SIZE: 3mm

YARN:

Green or pink

OTHER MATERIALS:

Toy filling

Cardboard

Ribbon, 30cm

Structure

The finished box piece should resemble a T-shape. The area indicated in the centre of the top-bar of the T-shape becomes the bottom of the box and the sections of fabric surrounding it are folded upwards along the dashed line. The vertical bar of the T-shape is folded around the remaining sides of the box.

Box

Using green or pink yarn, make a 37ch.

1st row: 1dc into the third ch from the hook, 1dc into each of next 35ch, turn. (36sts)

2nd-12th rows: 1ch (counts as first dc), 1 dc into each dc, turn.

Fasten off.

Rejoin yarn to 13th st from edge.

13th row: 1ch (counts as first dc), 1dc into next 11 sts, turn. (12sts)

14th–48th rows: 1ch (counts as first dc), 1dc into each dc, turn.

Fasten off.

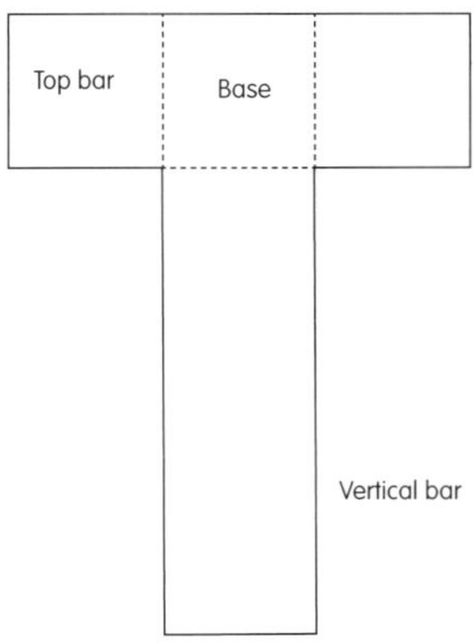

```
                       0 X X X X X X X X X X X
                       X X X X X X X X X X X 0
                       0 X X X X X X X X X X X
                       X X X X X X X X X X X 0
                       0 X X X X X X X X X X X
                       X X X X X X X X X X X 0
                       0 X X X X X X X X X X X
                       X X X X X X X X X X X 0
                       0 X X X X X X X X X X X
                       X X X X X X X X X X X 0
                       0 X X X X X X X X X X X
                       X X X X X X X X X X X 0
                       0 X X X X X X X X X X X
                       X X X X X X X X X X X 0
                       0 X X X X X X X X X X X
                       X X X X X X X X X X X 0
                       0 X X X X X X X X X X X
                       X X X X X X X X X X X 0
                       0 X X X X X X X X X X X
                       X X X X X X X X X X X 0
                       0 X X X X X X X X X X X
                       X X X X X X X X X X X 0
                       0 X X X X X X X X X X X
                       X X X X X X X X X X X 0
                       0 X X X X X X X X X X X
                       X X X X X X X X X X X 0
                       0 X X X X X X X X X X X
                       X X X X X X X X X X X 0
                       0 X X X X X X X X X X X
                       X X X X X X X X X X X 0
                       0 X X X X X X X X X X X
                       X X X X X X X X X X X 0
                       0 X X X X X X X X X X X
                       X X X X X X X X X X X 0
                       0 X X X X X X X X X X X
                       X X X X X X X X X X X 0
0 X X X X X X X X X X X X X X X X X X X X X X X X X X X X X X X X X X X
X X X X X X X X X X X X X X X X X X X X X X X X X X X X X X X X X X X 0
0 X X X X X X X X X X X X X X X X X X X X X X X X X X X X X X X X X X X
X X X X X X X X X X X X X X X X X X X X X X X X X X X X X X X X X X X 0
0 X X X X X X X X X X X X X X X X X X X X X X X X X X X X X X X X X X X
X X X X X X X X X X X X X X X X X X X X X X X X X X X X X X X X X X X 0
0 X X X X X X X X X X X X X X X X X X X X X X X X X X X X X X X X X X X
X X X X X X X X X X X X X X X X X X X X X X X X X X X X X X X X X X X 0
0 X X X X X X X X X X X X X X X X X X X X X X X X X X X X X X X X X X X
X X X X X X X X X X X X X X X X X X X X X X X X X X X X X X X X X X X 0
0 X X X X X X X X X X X X X X X X X X X X X X X X X X X X X X X X X X X
X X X X X X X X X X X X X X X X X X X X X X X X X X X X X X X X X X X 0
0 0 0 0 0 0 0 0 0 0 0 0 0 0 0 0 0 0 0 0 0 0 0 0 0 0 0 0 0 0 0 0 0 0 0 0
```

Making up

Using the photographs as reference and matching yarn, fold as indicated on structure diagram. Pin and stitch edges, leaving one edge open. If you want to stiffen the box slightly, cut out four squares of cardboard to fit each side of the cube, and slip these into the box so each rests against one side of the box. Stuff the box to hold the cardboard in place and stitch the opening closed. To finish, tie a length of ribbon around the box.

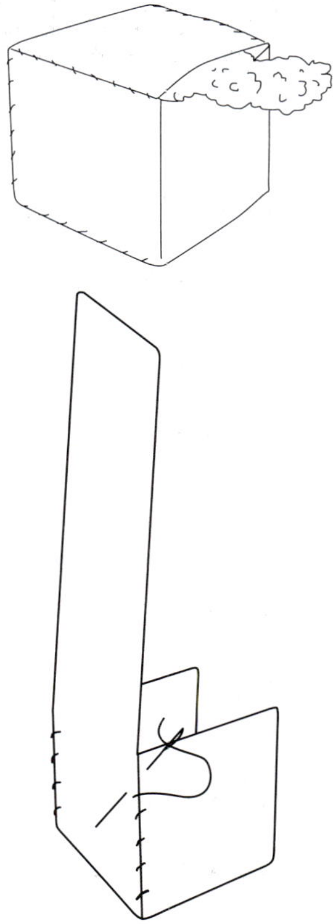

Happy Birthday Cake

No need to cut the cake or blow out the candles on this super birthday surprise. Create this creamy, crochet confection and you will have a real treat that keeps for every anniversary party.

Size

Height: 20cm

Materials

HOOK SIZE: 3MM

YARN:

White for the cakes

Cream for the candle

Pink for the candle

Brown for the chocolate decoration

Red for the cherries and flame

OTHER MATERIALS:

Toy filling

Cardboard

Structure

The birthday cake is made in two tiers using three pieces; bottom tier, bottom tier base and top tier.

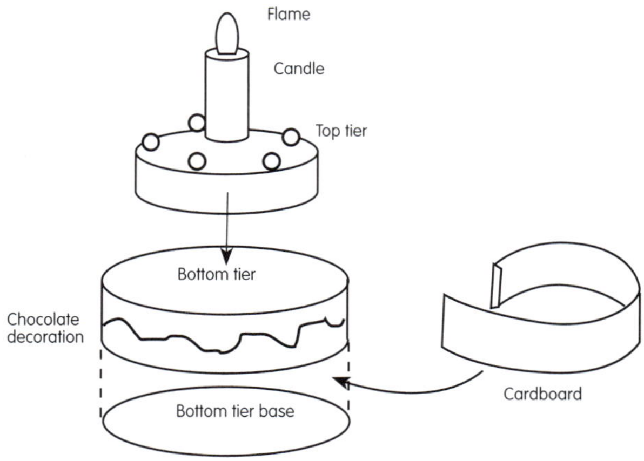

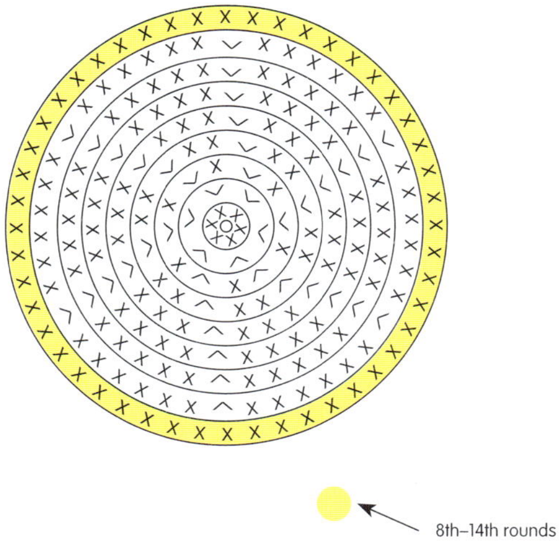

Bottom tier

Using white yarn, make a magic ring as follows.

Make a loop with tail end of yarn on right, keeping ball end on left. Pull the ball end through loop. Make one chain through loop on hook you have drawn through to steady the circle. Work 6dc into the circle and complete with sl st into the first dc. See also page 13.

1st round: 2dc into each dc. (12sts)

2nd round: [1dc into next dc, 2dc into foll 1dc] 6 times. (18sts)

3rd round: [1dc into each of next 2dc, 2dc into foll 1dc] 6 times. (24sts)

4th round: [1dc into each of next 3dc, 2dc into foll dc] 6 times. (30sts)

5th round: [1dc into each of next 4dc, 2dc into foll dc] 6 times. (36sts)

6th round: [1dc into each of next 5dc, 2dc into foll dc] 6 times. (42sts)

7th round: [1dc into each of next 6dc, 2dc into foll dc] 6 times. (48sts)

8th–14th rounds: 1dc into each dc.

Fasten off.

Bottom tier base

Using white yarn, make a magic ring as for the bottom tier.

1st round: 2dc into each dc. (12sts)

2nd round: [1dc into next dc, 2dc into foll 1dc] 6 times. (18sts)

3rd round: [1dc into each of next 2dc, 2dc into foll 1dc] 6 times. (24sts)

4th round: [1dc into each of next 3dc, 2dc into foll dc] 6 times. (30sts)

5th round: [1dc into each of next 4dc, 2dc into foll dc] 6 times. (36sts)

6th round: [1dc into each of next 5dc, 2dc into foll dc] 6 times. (42sts)

7th round: [1dc into each of next 6dc, 2dc into foll dc] 6 times. (48sts)

Fasten off.

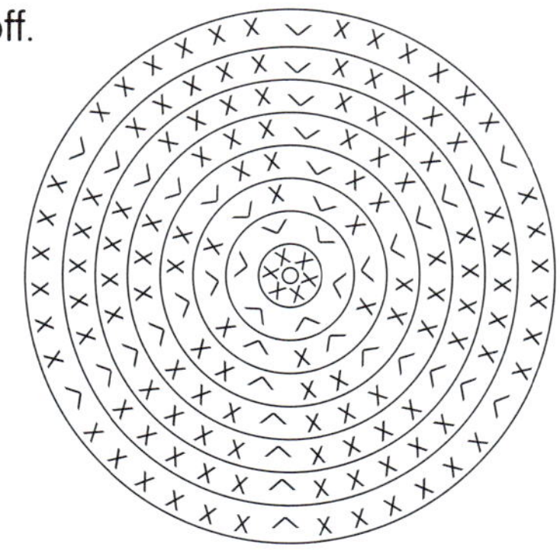

Top tier

Using white yarn, make a magic ring as for the bottom tier.

1st round: 2dc into each dc. (12sts)

2nd round: [1dc into next dc, 2dc into foll 1dc] 6 times. (18sts)

3rd round: [1dc into each of next 2dc, 2dc into foll 1dc] 6 times. (24sts)

4th round: [1dc into each of next 3dc, 2dc into foll dc] 6 times. (30sts)

5th round: [1dc into each of next 4dc, 2dc into foll dc] 6 times. (36sts)

6th–12th rounds: 1dc into each dc.

Fasten off.

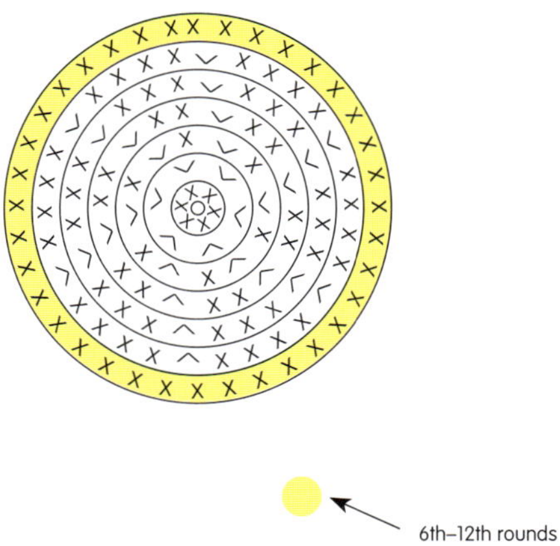

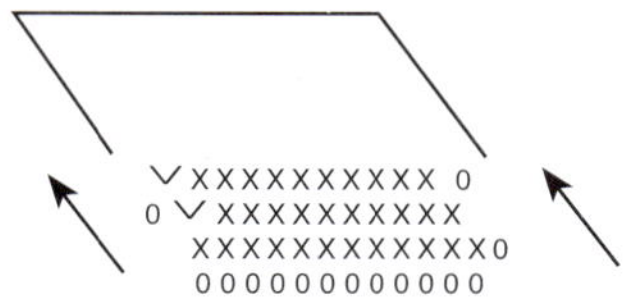

Candle

Using cream yarn, make 13ch.

1st row: 1dc into the second ch from the hook, 1dc into each ch, turn.

2nd row: 1ch, 2dc into first st, 1dc into each of next 10dc, turn.

Join in pink yarn.

3rd row: 1ch, skip 1dc, 1dc into each of next 10dc, 2dc into the last st, turn.

4th row: 1ch, 2dc into first st, 1dc into each of next 10dc, turn.

5th row: Using in cream yarn, 1ch, skip 1dc, 1dc into each of next 10dc, 2dc into the last st, turn.

6th row: 1ch, 2dc into first st, 1dc into each of next 10dc, turn.

Repeat the last 4 rows twice more.

Repeat 3rd–4th rows once more.

Fasten off.

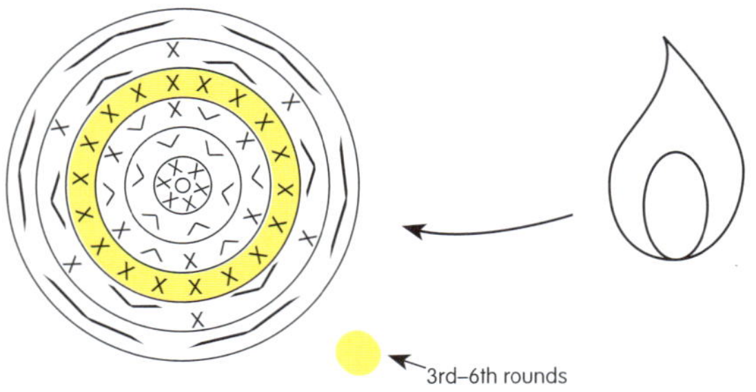

Flame

Using red yarn, make a magic ring as for the bottom tier.

1st round: 2dc into each dc. (12sts)

2nd round: [1dc into next dc, 2dc into foll 1dc] 6 times. (18sts)

3rd–6th rounds: 1dc into each dc.

7th round: [1dc into next dc, dc2tog] 6 times. (12sts)

8th round: [dc2tog] 6 times. (6sts)

Fasten off.

Chocolate decoration

4tr-bobble = [wrap the yarn around the hook, insert the hook into fourth ch from hook, wrap yarn around hook, draw yarn through ch, wrap yarn around hook draw yarn through two loops on hook] 4 times, wrap yarn around hook draw yarn through all loops on the hook.

Using brown yarn, make 4ch.

1st row: 4tr-bobble [4ch, 4tr-bobble] 30 times or as many times as you wish to wrap around the bottom tier.

Fasten off.

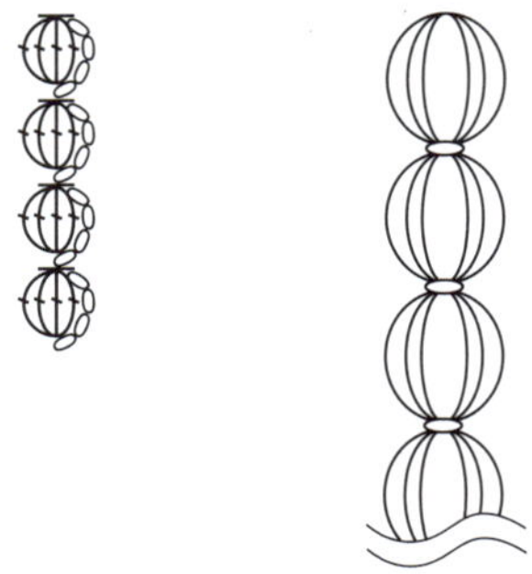

Cherries (make 5)

Using red yarn, make a magic ring as for the bottom tier.

1st round: 2dc into each dc. (12sts)

2nd–5th rounds: 1dc into each dc.

Fasten off and use the yarn tail to gather the edge.

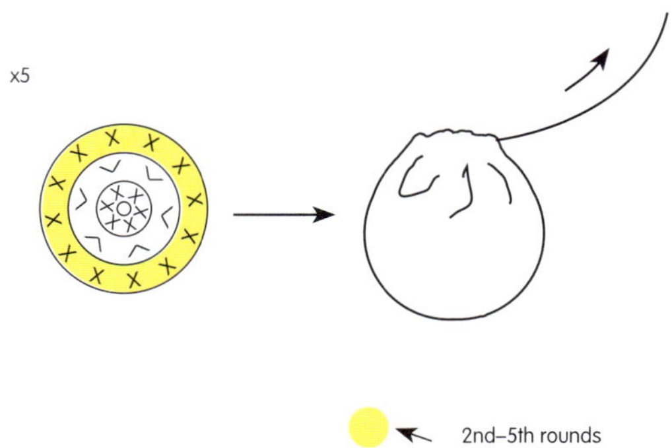

Making up

Cut a length of cardboard equal to the circumference of the bottom tier. Position the cardboard inside the bottom tier against the sides and hold in place with toy filling. Stitch the base to the bottom tier. Pin the top tier to the bottom tier, partially stitch in place, stuff the top tier with toy filling and complete the seam.

Stitch the edge of the first row and the edge of the last row of the candle together. Cut the cardboard to match the length of the candle and roll it into a cylinder shape. Place the cardboard roll and toy filling into the candle body. Gather the top edge and secure. Stitch the flame in place.

Using the photographs as reference and matching yarn, stitch the candle and the cherries to the top tier, and the chocolate decoration to the bottom tier.

This is one candle no one will be able to blow out!

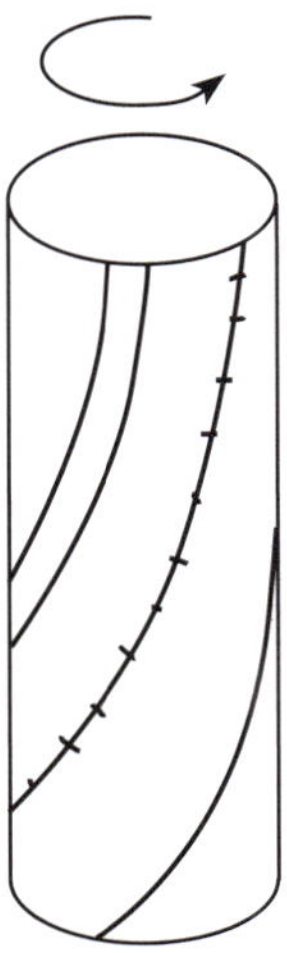

Hooray Bubbles!

When there's something to celebrate – whatever the occasion – it's time to break out the bubbles. So have some fun with the fizz, and see if you can pop the cork on this charming champagne surprise.

Size

Height: 25cm

Materials

HOOK SIZE: 3mm

YARN:

Green for the bottle

White for the label

Brown for the ribbon

Red for the seal

Gold Lurex or sparkly yarn for the foil

Yellow for the foil

OTHER MATERIALS:

Toy filling

Structure

Champagne bottle is made with two sections.

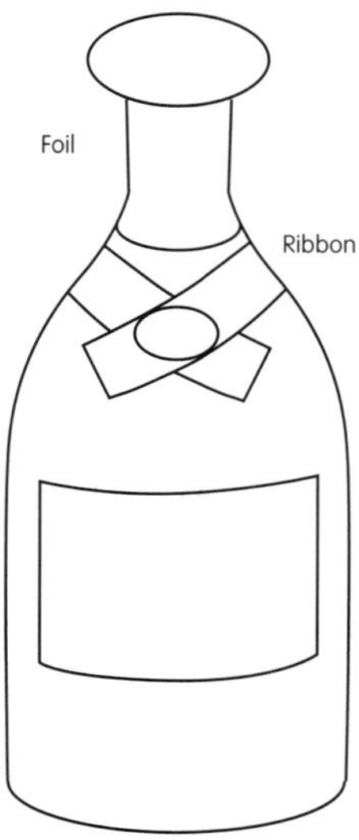

BRUT
VINTAGE
2008
Freixenet
EXCELENCIA
CAVA

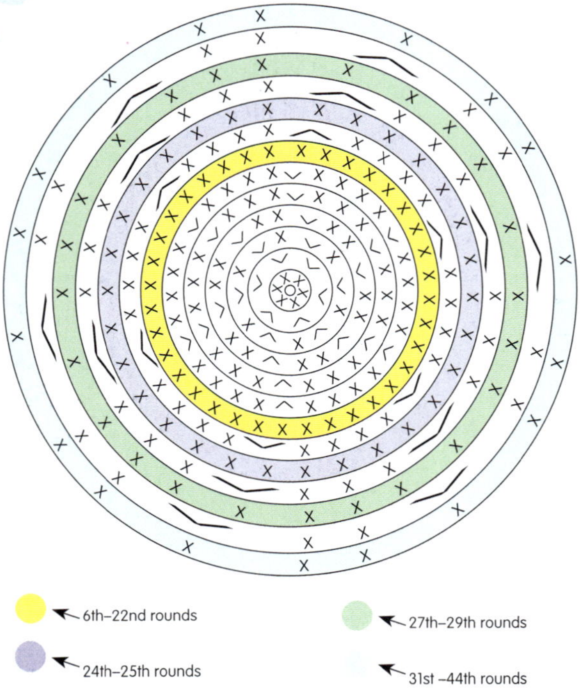

Bottle

Using green yarn, make a magic ring as follows.

Make a loop with tail end of yarn on right, keeping ball end on left. Pull the ball end through loop. Make one chain through loop on hook you have drawn through to steady the circle. Work 6dc into the circle and complete with sl st into the first dc. See also page 13.

1st round: 2dc into each dc. (12sts)

2nd round: [1dc into next dc, 2dc into foll 1dc] 6 times. (18sts)

3rd round: [1dc into each of next 2dc, 2dc into foll 1dc] 6 times. (24sts)

4th round: [1dc into each of next 3dc, 2dc into foll dc] 6 times. (30sts)

5th round: [1dc into each of next 4dc, 2dc into foll dc] 6 times. (36sts)

6th–22nd rounds: 1dc into each dc.

23rd round: [1dc into each of next 4dc, dc2tog] 6 times. (30sts)

24th–25th rounds: 1dc into each dc.

26th round: [1dc into each of next 3dc, dc2tog] 6 times. (24sts)

27th–28th rounds: 1dc into each dc.

Fasten off green yarn, join in yellow and gold Lurex double stranded.

29th round: 1dc into each dc.

30th round: [1dc into each of next 2dc, dc2tog] 6 times. (18sts)

31st–44th rounds: 1dc into each dc.

Fasten off.

Foil

Using yellow and gold Lurex yarn stranded together, make a magic ring as for the bottle.

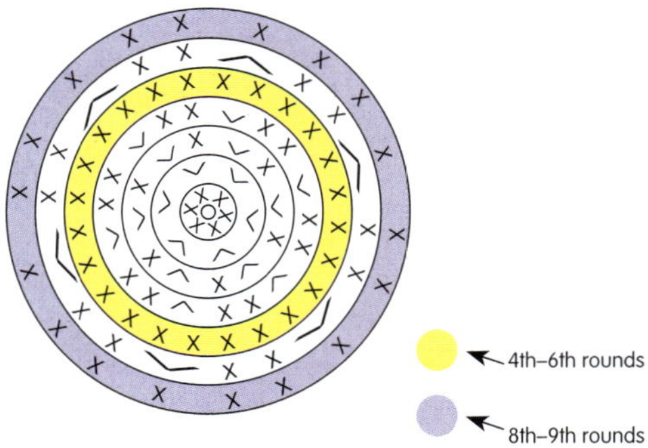

1st round: 2dc into each dc. (12sts)

2nd round: [1dc into next dc, 2dc into foll dc] 6 times. (18sts)

3rd round: [1dc into each of next 2dc, 2dc into foll dc] 6 times. (24sts)

4th–6th rounds: 1dc into each dc.

7th round: [1dc into each of next 2dc, dc2tog] 6 times. (18sts)

8th–9th rounds: 1dc into each dc.

Fasten off.

Ribbon

Using brown yarn, make 8ch.

1st row: 1htr into the third ch from the hook, 1htr into each ch, turn. (6sts)

2nd row: 2ch (counts as first htr), 1htr into the back loop of each dc, turn.

Repeat the last row until the ribbon is long enough to go around the neck of the bottle.

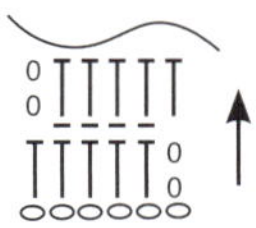

Seal

Using red yarn, make a magic ring as for the bottle.

1st round: 2dc into each dc. (12sts)

2nd round: [1dc into next dc, 2dc into foll dc] 6 times. (18sts)

Fasten off.

Label

Using brown yarn, make 18ch.

1st row: 1htr into the third ch from the hook, 1htr into each ch, turn. (16sts)

2nd–7th rows: 2ch (counts as first htr), 1htr into the back loop of each dc, turn.

Making up

Using the structure diagram and photographs as reference, stuff and assemble the bottle and foil pieces. Stitch the ribbon, seal and label in place and perhaps embroider a name onto the label for a champagne shower of appreciation!

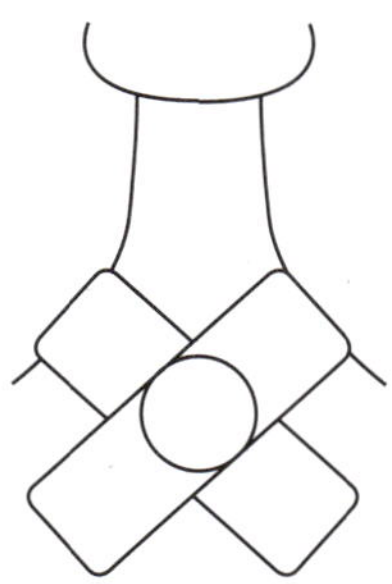

Time to Party!

When the long, hot days of summer arrive it's time to get out in the garden and bring out the barbie. So whip up a quick crocheted kebab and a corn-on-the-cob to celebrate while the sun shines.

Size

Cob of corn length: 6cm

Onion width: 7cm

Meat chunk and tomato width: 6cm

Pepper length: 6.5cm

Materials

HOOK SIZE: 3mm

YARN:

Yellow and cream for the cob of corn

Cream and brown for the onion

Brown for the meat

Red for the tomato

Green for the pepper

OTHER MATERIALS:

Toy filling

Wooden skewer

Structure of Cob of corn

Sweet corn is made of the corn and two cob end pieces.

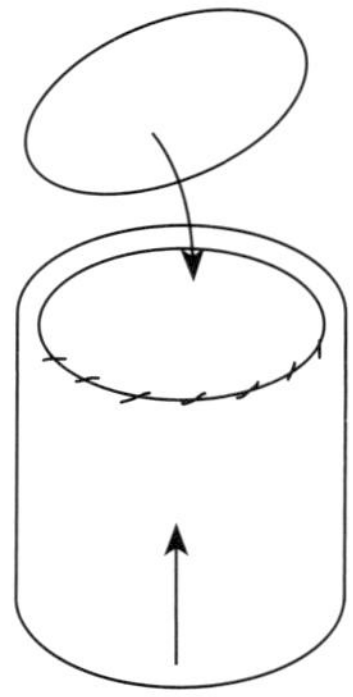

Corn

Using yellow yarn, make a magic ring as follows.

Make a loop with tail end of yarn on right, keeping ball end on left. Pull the ball end through loop. Make one chain through loop on hook you have drawn through to steady the circle. Work 6dc into the circle and complete with sl st into the first dc. See also page 13.

1st round: 2dc into each dc. (12sts)

2nd round: [1dc into next dc, 2dc into foll 1dc] 6 times. (18sts)

3rd round: [1dc into each of next 2dc, 2dc into foll 1dc] 6 times. (24sts)

4th round: [1dc into each of next 3dc, 2dc into foll dc] 6 times. (30sts)

5th–12th rounds: 1dc into each dc.

13th round: [1dc into each of next 3dc, dc2tog] 6 times. (24sts)

14th round: [1dc into each of next 2dc, dc2tog] 6 times. (18sts)

Stuff the corn with toy filling.

15th round: [1dc into next dc, dc2tog] 6 times. (12sts)

16th round: [dc2tog] 6 times. (6sts)

Fasten off.

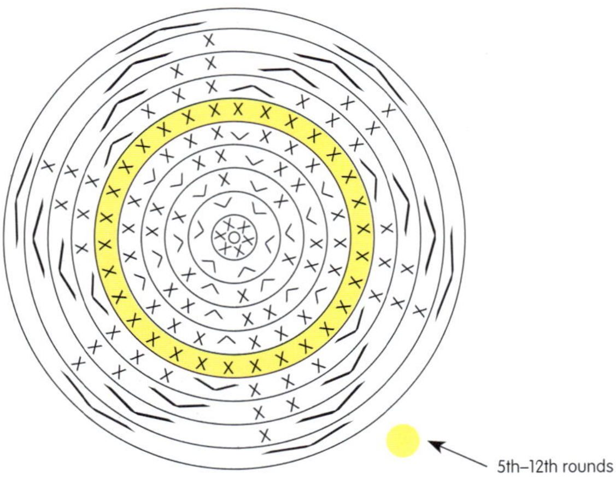

Cob end (make 2)

Using cream yarn, make a magic ring as for the corn.

Work as for legs until 3rd round.

Fasten off.

Making up

Using the structure diagram and photographs as reference, assemble the corn and cob end pieces.

Onion

Using cream yarn, make a magic ring as for the corn.

1st round: 2dc into each dc. (12sts)

2nd round: [1dc into next dc, 2dc into foll 1dc] 6 times. (18sts)

3rd round: [1dc into each of next 2dc, 2dc into foll 1dc] 6 times. (24sts)

4th round: [1dc into each of next 3dc, 2dc into foll dc] 6 times. (30sts)

Fasten off.

Making up

Using the photographs as reference, fold the roundel in half and using brown yarn, embroider concentric lines of straight stitches.

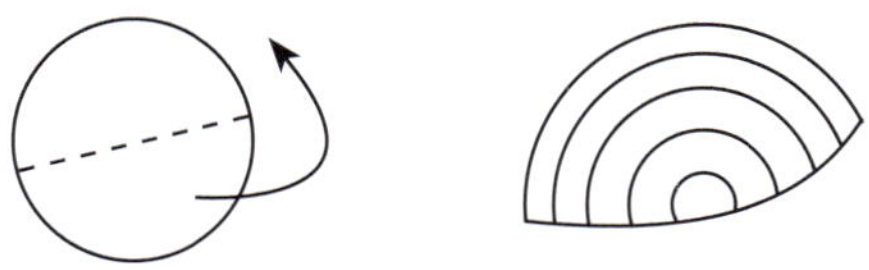

Tomato

Using red yarn, make a magic ring as for the corn.

Work as for the onion.

Using the photographs as reference, fold the roundel in half and stitch the edges.

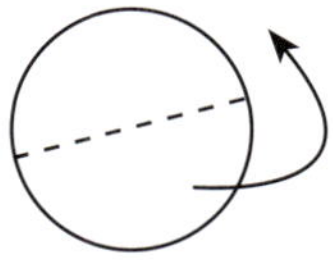

Meat

Using brown yarn, make a magic ring as for the corn.

1st round: 2dc into each dc. (12sts)

2nd round: [1dc into next dc, 2dc into foll 1dc] 6 times. (18sts)

3rd round: [1dc into each of next 2dc, 2dc into foll 1dc] 6 times. (24sts)

4th round: [1dc into each of next 3dc, 2dc into foll dc] 6 times. (30sts)

5th–12th rounds: 1dc into each dc.

Fasten off.

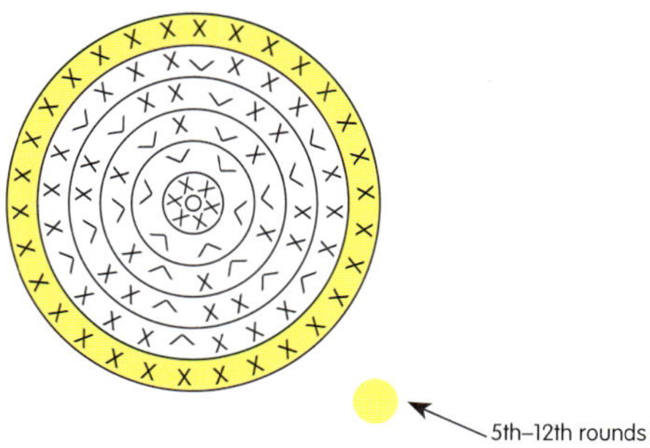

Making up

Using the photographs as reference, flatten the cylinder and using brown yarn, embroider random long parallel straight stitches to make it look like well-grilled meat!

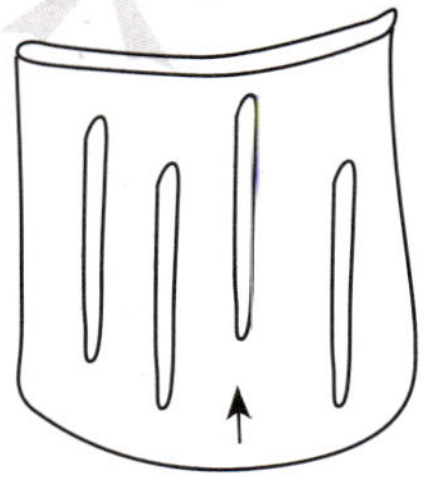

Green pepper

Using green yarn, make 16ch.

1st row: 1dc into the second ch from the hook, 1dc into each ch to end. (15sts)

2nd–5th rows: 1ch, 1dc into the back loop of each dc.

Fasten off.

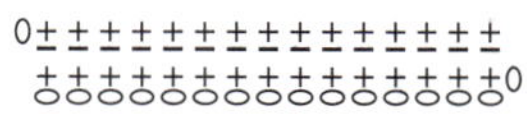

Making up

Using the photographs as reference, fold the rectangle in half lengthways and stitch neighbouring short edges together.

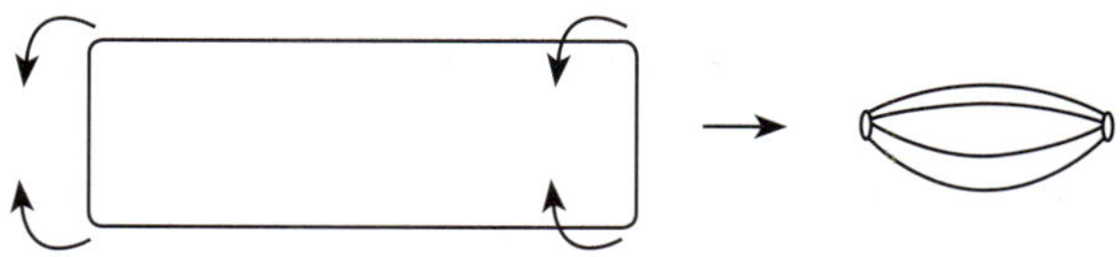

Finishing

Place all the yummy vegetables and meat onto a wooden skewer.

Chapter 5

Congratulations!

Oh So Clever!

If one of your friends or family is a real brain box then be sure to reward their academic achievement. So when it's time to dish out the diplomas, celebrate exam success with this wise little owl.

Size

Height: 12.5cm

Materials

HOOK SIZE: 3mm

YARN:

Pale brown for the head, body and ears

White and pale blue for the eyes

Yellow for the beak

Purple mohair yarn for the tummy

Black for the hat

OTHER MATERIALS:

Toy filling

2 mismatched toy safety eyes, 8mm

Structure

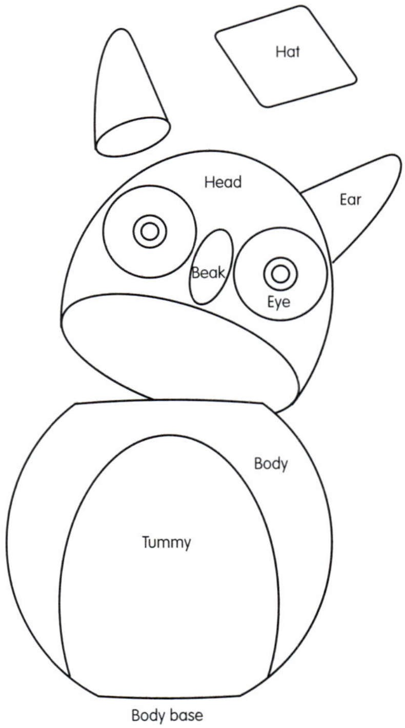

Head

Using pale brown yarn, make a magic ring as follows.

Make a loop with tail end of yarn on right, keeping ball end on left. Pull the ball end through loop. Make one chain through loop on hook you have drawn through to steady the circle. Work 6dc into the circle and complete with sl st into the first dc. See also page 13.

1st round: 2dc into each dc. (12sts)

2nd round: [1dc into next dc, 2dc into foll 1dc] 6 times. (18sts)

3rd round: [1dc into each of next 2dc, 2dc into foll 1dc] 6 times. (24sts)

4th round: [1dc into each of next 3dc, 2dc into foll dc] 6 times. (30sts)

5th round: [1dc into each of next 4dc, 2dc into foll dc] 6 times. (36sts)

6th–15th rounds: 1dc into each dc.

Fasten off.

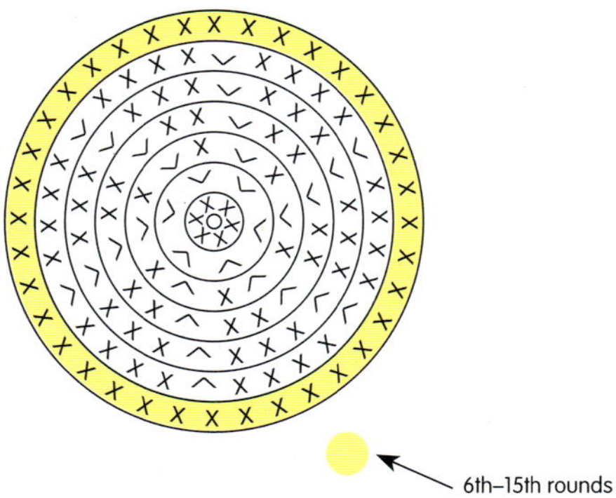

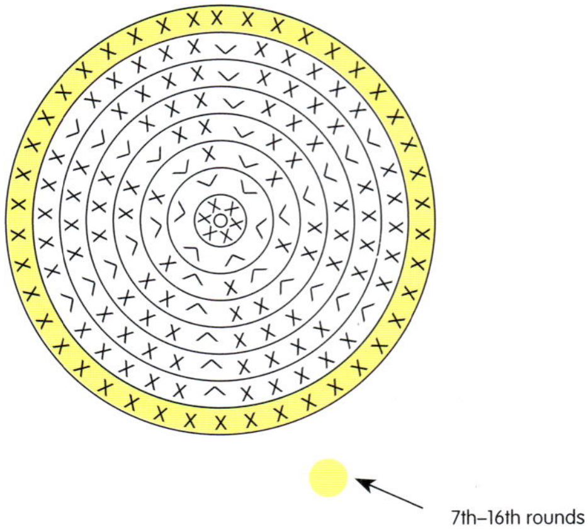

Body

Using pale brown yarn, make a magic ring as for the head.

1st round: 2dc into each dc. (12sts)

2nd round: [1dc into next dc, 2dc into foll dc] 6 times. (18sts)

3rd round: [1dc into each of next 2dc, 2dc into foll dc] 6 times. (24sts)

4th round: [1dc into each of next 3dc, 2dc into foll dc] 6 times. (30sts)

5th round: [1dc into each of next 4dc, 2dc into foll dc] 6 times. (36sts)

6th round: [1dc into each of next 5dc, 2dc into foll dc] 6 times. (42sts)

7th–16th rounds: 1dc into each dc.

Fasten off.

Eyes (make 2)

Using white yarn, make a magic ring as for the head.

Fasten off white yarn and join in pale blue yarn.

1st round: 2dc into each dc. (12sts)

2nd round: [1dc into next dc, 2dc into foll dc] 6 times. (18sts)

Fasten off.

x2

Ears (make 2)

Using pale brown yarn, make a magic ring as for the head.

1st–2nd rounds: 1dc into each dc. (6sts)

3rd round: 2dc into each dc. (12sts)

4th round: [1dc into next dc, 2dc into foll dc] 6 times. (18sts)

5th–7th rounds: 1dc into each dc.

x2

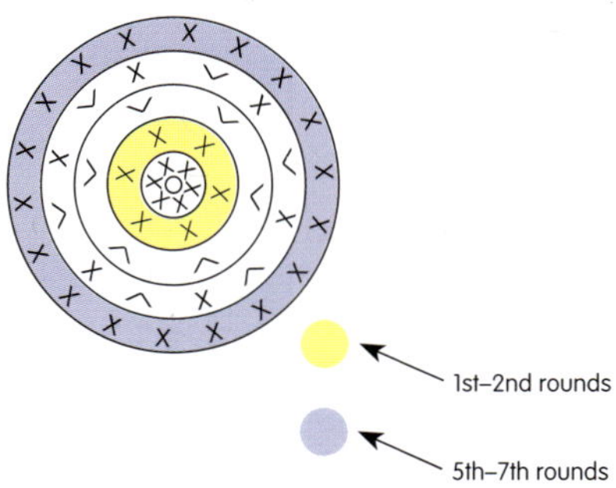

Tummy

Using purple mohair yarn, make a magic ring as for the head.

1st round: 2dc into each dc. (12sts)

2nd round: [1dc into next dc, 2dc into foll dc] 6 times. (18sts)

3rd round: [1dc into each of next 2dc, 2dc into foll dc] 6 times. (24sts)

4th round: [1dc into each of next 3dc, 2dc into foll dc] 6 times. (30sts)

5th round: [1dc into each of next 4dc, 2dc into foll dc] 6 times. (36sts)

Fasten off.

Beak

Using yellow yarn, make 7ch.

1st row: 1dc into the second ch from the hook, 1dc into each ch to end, turn. (6sts)

2nd row: 1ch, skip the st at the base of the ch, 1dc into each of next 5dc turn. (5sts)

3rd row: 1ch, skip the st at the base of the ch, 1dc into each of next 4dc, turn. (4sts)

4th row: 1ch, skip the st at the base of the ch, 1dc into each of next 3dc, turn. (3sts)

5th row: 1ch, skip the st at the base of the ch, 1dc into each of next 2dc, turn. (2sts)

6th row: 1ch, skip the st at the base of the ch, 1dc into next 1dc, turn. (1st)

Fasten off.

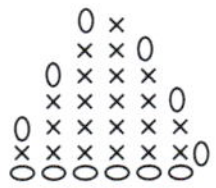

Fold the beak in half along the chain edge and stitch the selvedge edges together.

Hat

Using black yarn, make 8ch.

1st row: 1htr into the third ch from the hook (counts as first htr), 1htr into each ch to end, turn. (7sts)

2nd row: 2ch, 1htr into each of next 6dc turn.

Repeat the last row until the length measures twice the width.

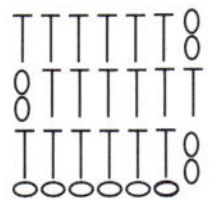

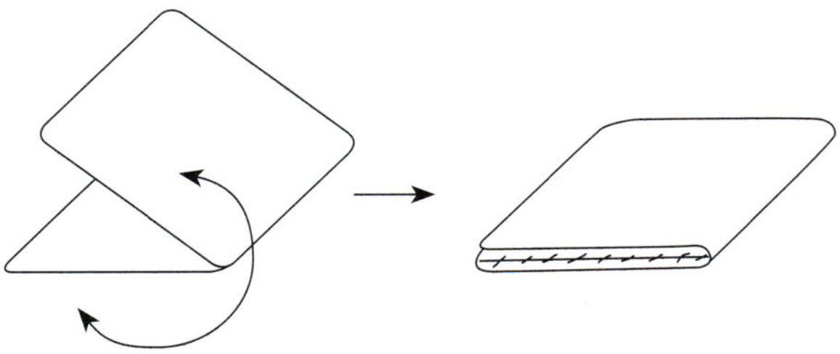

Fold in half lengthways and stitch the selvedge edges together.

Making up

Attach the toy safety eyes. Using the photographs as reference and matching yarn, stuff the head and body and attach the head to the body. Stitch the ears, eyes and beak to the face and the hat between the ears. Finally, stitch the tummy to the body and make it look like the clever little owl it is!

Cute Little Baby

When the stork brings that special bundle of joy, it's time to welcome the new arrival with pretty little presents. So why not make the bouncing baby their very own mini-me?

Size

Height: 10cm

Materials

HOOK SIZE: 3mm

YARN:

Flesh-coloured for the head

White for the dummy and bib

Dark pink for the body and bib

Light pink for the cheeks

Yellow for the hair

OTHER MATERIALS:

Toy filling

Black beads, 4mm

Head

Using flesh-coloured yarn, make a magic ring as follows.

Make a loop with tail end of yarn on right, keeping ball end on left. Pull the ball end through loop. Make one chain through loop on hook you have drawn through to steady the circle. Work 6dc into the circle and complete with sl st into the first dc. See also page 13.

1st round: 2dc into each dc. (12sts)

2nd round: [1dc into next dc, 2dc into foll 1dc] 6 times. (18sts)

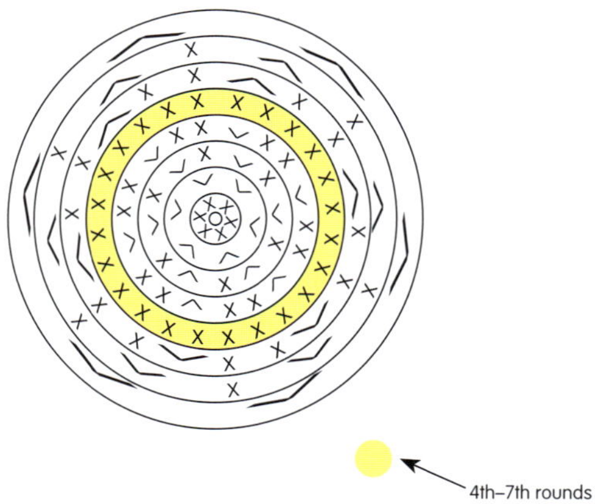

3rd round: [1dc into each of next 2dc, 2dc into foll 1dc] 6 times. (24sts)

4th–7th rounds: 1dc into each dc.

8th round: [1dc into each of next 2dc, dc2tog] 6 times. (18sts)

Stuff the head with toy filling.

9th round: [1dc into next dc, dc2tog] 6 times. (12sts)

10th round: [dc2tog] 6 times. (6sts)

Fasten off.

Body

Using dark pink yarn, make a magic ring as for the head.

1st round: 2dc into each dc. (12sts)

2nd round: [1dc into next dc, 2dc into foll dc] 6 times. (18sts)

3rd round: 1dc into each dc.

Repeat the last round until the piece measures 3cm.

Fasten off.

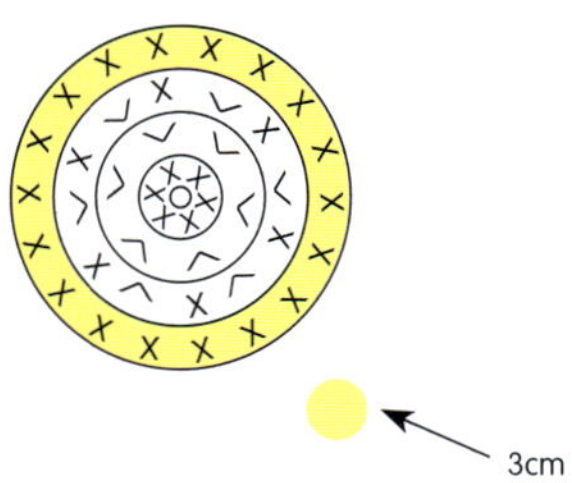

Legs (make 2)

Using dark pink yarn, make a magic ring as for the head.

1st round: 1dc into each dc. (6sts)

Repeat the last round until the piece measures 3cm.

Fasten off.

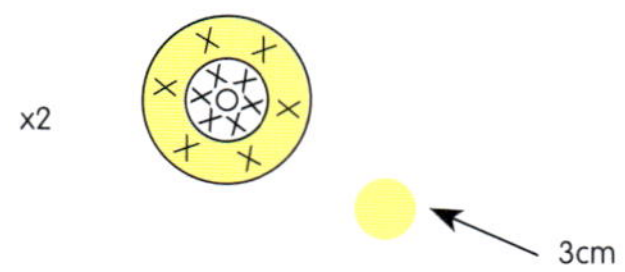

Arms (make 2)

Using dark pink yarn, make a magic ring as for the head.

1st round: 1dc into each dc. (6sts)

Repeat the last round until the piece measures 2cm.

Fasten off.

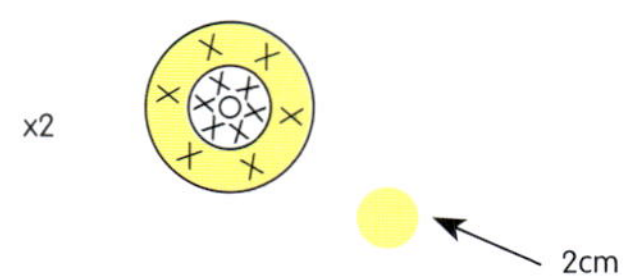

Bib

Using white yarn, make a magic ring as for the head.

1st round: 2dc into each dc. (12sts)

Fasten off white yarn. Join in dark pink yarn to any dc.

2nd round: 1ch, 1dc into dc at base of ch, [2dc into the next dc, 1dc into foll dc] 4 times.

Fasten off.

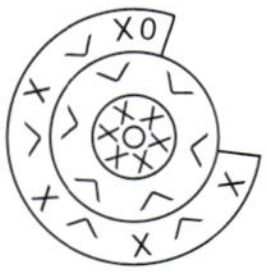

Cheeks (make 2)

Using light pink yarn, make a magic ring as for the head.

Fasten off.

x2

Dummy

Using white yarn, make a magic ring as for the head.

1st round: 1dc into each dc. (6sts)

Fasten off.

Making up

Using the photographs as reference and matching yarn, stitch the cheeks, dummy and the black beads (for the eyes) in place. Using yellow yarn, embroider a chain stitch curl on to the head to represent hair. Stitch the head, arms, legs and bib to the body and a new amigurumi child is born!

What a Winner!

At moments of personal triumph, who doesn't want to feel like a complete winner? Let someone know that they're really special – whatever the event – with their very own gold medal and trophy.

Gold Trophy

Size

Height: 16cm

Materials

HOOK SIZE: 3mm

YARN:

Yellow for the main trophy sections

Dark yellow for the decoration

OTHER MATERIALS:

Toy filling

Cardboard

Structure

The gold trophy is worked in five sections.

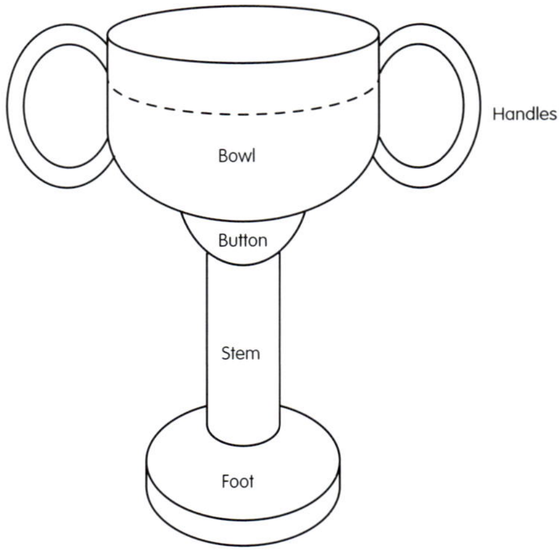

Bowl

Using yellow yarn, make a magic ring as follows.

Make a loop with tail end of yarn on right, keeping ball end on left. Pull the ball end through loop. Make one chain through loop on hook you have drawn through to steady the circle. Work 6dc into the circle and complete with sl st into the first dc. See also page 13.

1st round: 2dc into each dc. (12sts)

2nd round: [1dc into next dc, 2dc into foll 1dc] 6 times. (18sts)

3rd round: [1dc into each of next 2dc, 2dc into foll 1dc] 6 times. (24sts)

4th round: [1dc into each of next 3dc, 2dc into foll 1dc] 6 times. (30sts)

5th round: [1dc into each of next 4dc, 2dc into foll 1dc] 6 times. (36sts)

6th round: 1dc into each dc.

7th round: [1dc into each of next 5dc, 2dc into foll 1dc] 6 times. (42sts)

8th round: 1dc into each dc.

9th round: [1dc into each of next 6dc, 2dc into foll 1dc] 6 times. (48sts)

10th–23rd rounds: 1dc into each dc.

Fasten off.

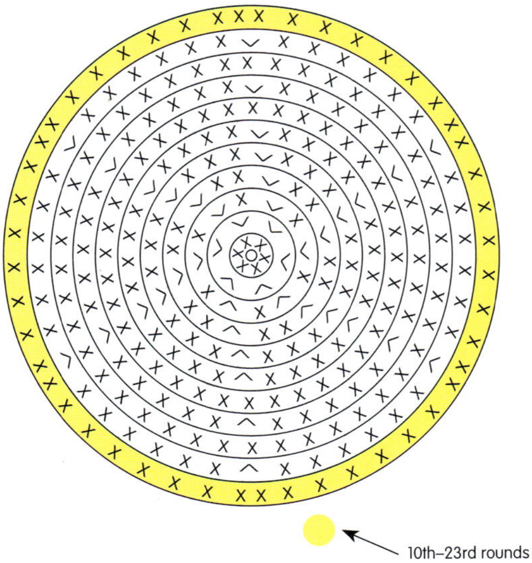

Button

Using yellow yarn, make a magic ring as for the bowl.

1st round: 2dc into each dc. (12sts)

2nd round: [1dc into next dc, 2dc into foll dc] 6 times. (18sts)

3rd round: [1dc into next 2dc, 2dc into foll dc] 6 times. (24sts)

4th–7th rounds: 1dc into each dc.

Fasten off.

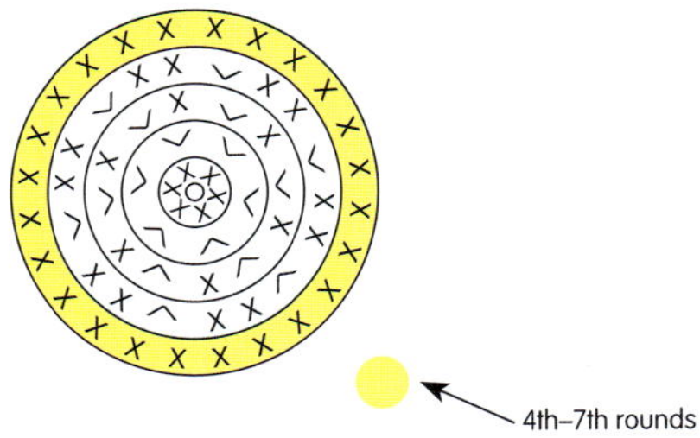

Stem

Using yellow yarn, make a magic ring as for the bowl.

1st round: 2dc into each dc. (12sts)

2nd round: [1dc into next dc, 2dc into foll dc] 6 times. (18sts)

3rd round: 1dc into each dc.

Repeat the last round until the work measures 10cm.

Fasten off.

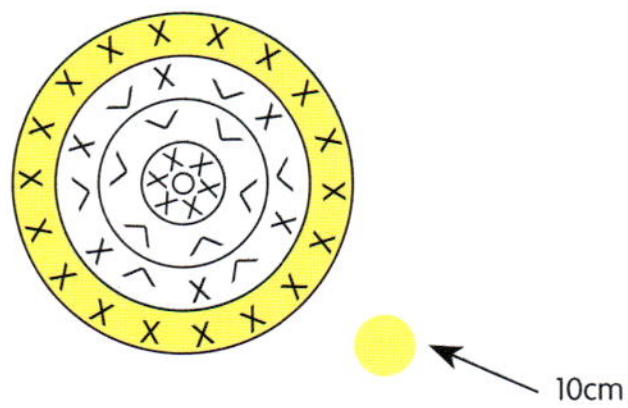

Foot

Using yellow yarn, make a magic ring as for the bowl.

1st round: 2dc into each dc. (12sts)

2nd round: [1dc into next dc, 2dc into foll dc] 6 times. (18sts)

3rd round: [1dc into each of next 2dc, 2dc into foll dc] 6 times. (24sts)

4th round: [1dc into each of next 3dc, 2dc into foll dc] 6 times. (30sts)

Measure and cut out a circle of cardboard to match the diameter of the work.

5th round: [1dc into each of next 3dc, dc2tog] 6 times. (24sts)

6th round: [1dc into each of next 2dc, dc2tog] 6 times. (18sts)

7th round: [1dc into next dc, dc2tog] 6 times. (12sts)

8th round: [dc2tog] 6 times. (6sts)

Fasten off.

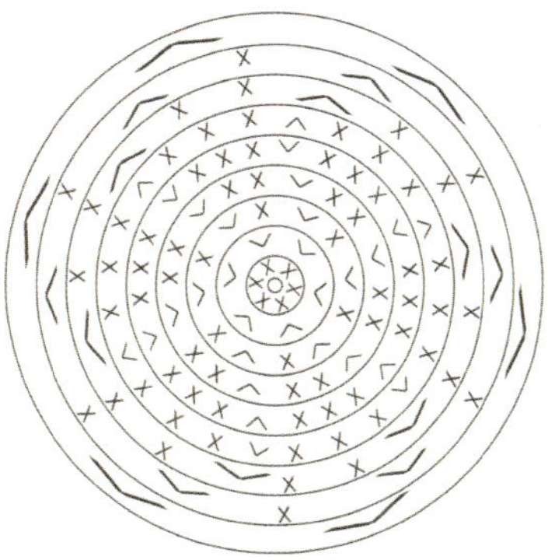

Handle (make 2)

Using yellow yarn, make a magic ring as for the bowl.

1st round: 2dc into each dc. (12sts)

2nd round: [1dc into next dc, 2dc into foll dc] 6 times. (18sts)

3rd round: 1dc into each dc.

Repeat the last row until the work measures 18cm or the length required.

Fasten off.

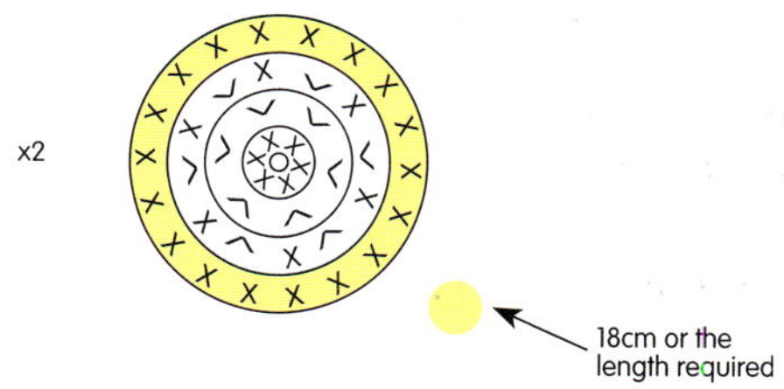

Leaf decoration (make 2)

4tr-bobble = [wrap the yarn around the hook, insert the hook into fourth ch from hook, wrap yarn around hook, draw yarn through ch, wrap yarn around hook draw yarn through two loops on hook] 4 times, wrap yarn around hook draw yarn through all loops on the hook.

Using dark yellow yarn, make 4ch

1st row: 4tr-bobble [4ch, 4tr-bobble] 13 times or as many times as you wish to twist around the handle.

Fasten off.

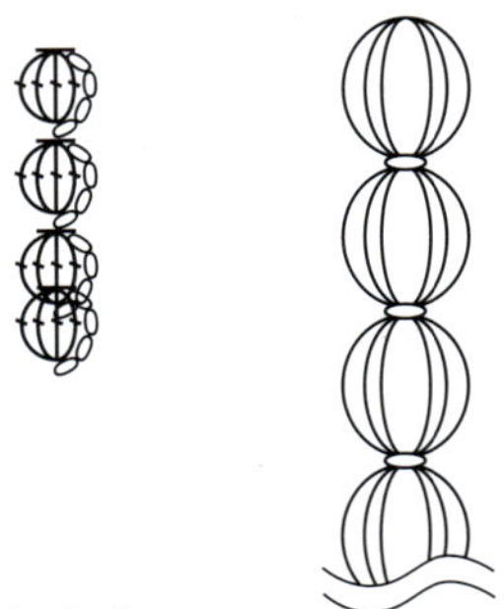

Making up

Cut the cardboard to match the length of the stem and roll it into a cylinder shape. Insert the cardboard roll and toy filling into the stem.

Cut the cardboard 3cm deep and to match the circumference of the bowl and twist it into a ring shape. Insert the ring into the bowl and fold the top edge over to cover the cardboard. Stitch in place.

Stuff the button and lightly stuff the handles with toy filling.

Using the photographs as reference and matching yarn, attach the foot to the stem, the stem to the button and the button to the bowl. Then, stitch the top of each handle to the lip of the bowl and shape and stitch the lower handle in place. Arrange the lengths of leaf decoration and stitch in place. What a winner!

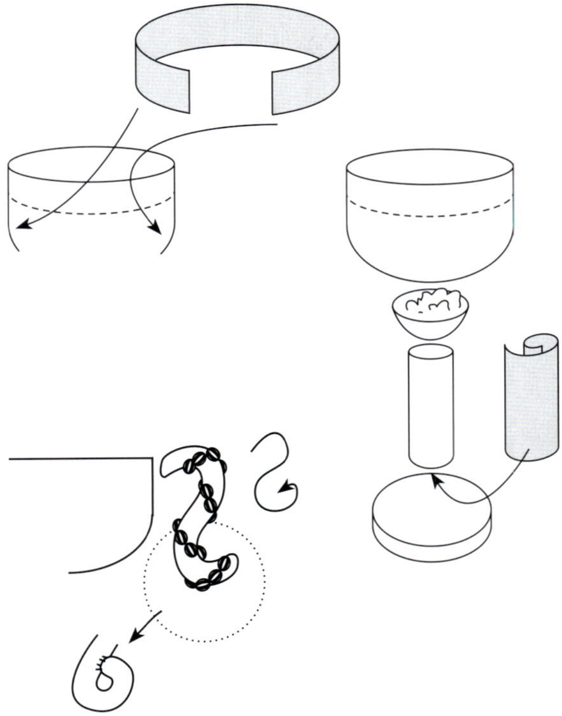

Gold medal

Size

Disc width: 9cm

Materials

HOOK SIZE: 3mm

YARN:

Yellow for the medal

Dark yellow for the medal decoration

Blue, white and red for the ribbon

OTHER MATERIALS:

Toy filling

Medal (make 2)

Using yellow yarn, make a magic ring as follows.

Make a loop with tail end of yarn on right, keeping ball end on left. Pull the ball end through loop. Make one chain through loop on hook you have drawn through to steady the circle. Work 6dc into the circle and complete with sl st into the first dc. See also page 13.

1st round: 2dc into each dc. (12sts)

2nd round: [1dc into next dc, 2dc into foll 1dc] 6 times. (18sts)

3rd round: [1dc into each of next 2dc, 2dc into foll 1dc] 6 times. (24sts)

4th round: [1dc into each of next 3dc, 2dc into foll dc] 6 times. (30sts)

5th round: [1dc into each of next 4dc, 2dc into foll dc] 6 times. (36sts)

6th–7th rounds: 1dc into each dc.

Fasten off.

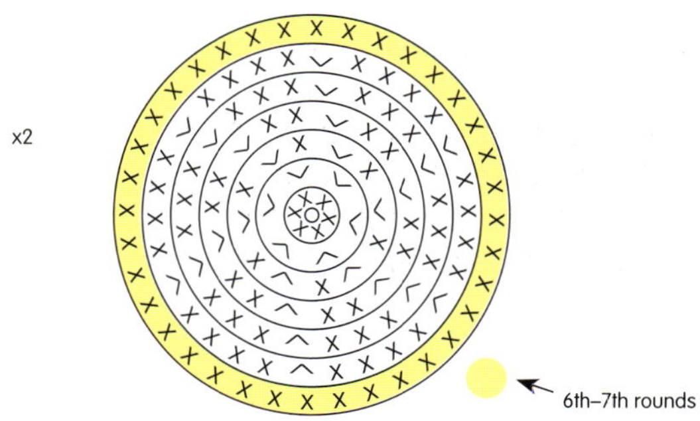

Leafy decoration (make 2)

Using dark yellow yarn, make 26ch.

1st row: Sl st into the fifth ch from the hook, sl st into next ch, [5ch, sl st into base of 5-ch, sl st into next ch] 10 times.

Do not work the remaining ch.

Fasten off.

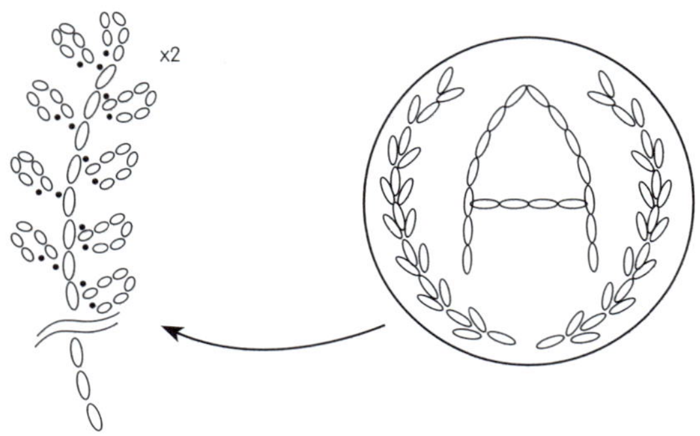

Letter or motif

Draw a life size cartoon of the letter or motif and divide into sections that can be crocheted.

Using dark yellow yarn, make a ch long enough for the first section of the letter

1st row: 1dc into the second ch from the hook, 1dc into each ch to end.

Fasten off.

Repeat for each section of the letter or motif.

For curves, work two double crochet stitches into the same stitch as required.

Ribbon

Using red yarn, make a ch long enough to fit around the neck.

1st row: 1htr into the third ch from the hook, 1htr into each ch to end.

Fasten off red yarn, join in white yarn.

2nd row: 2ch, 1htr into each htr.

Fasten off white yarn, join in blue yarn.

3rd row: 2ch, 1htr into each htr.

Fasten off.

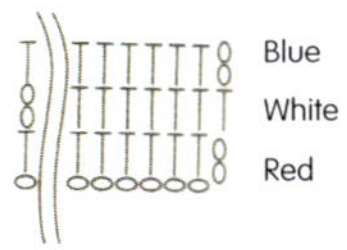

Making up

Place the two medal pieces on top of each other with your preferred side facing out. Using matching yarn, sew the two pieces together around most of the outer edge, fill with toy stuffing and complete the seam.

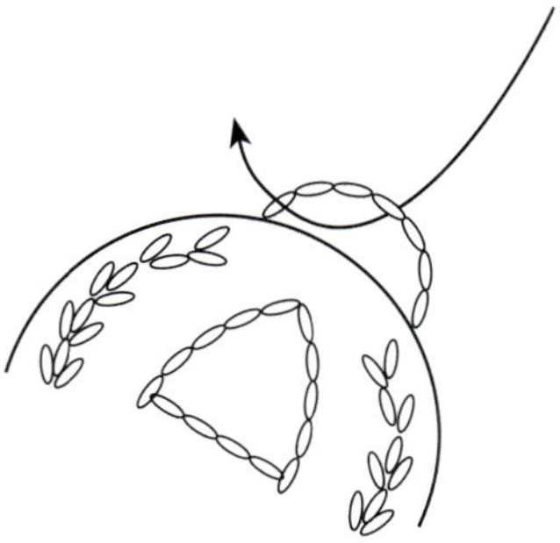

Then, using the photographs as reference, attach the leaf decoration and any other motif you may have crocheted.

Using yellow yarn, join in to the top of the medal about 1.5cm to the right of the centre top, make a ch long enough to reach a point about 1.5cm to the right of the centre top and sl st through the seam stitches at this point. Turn, 1ch, work dc sts around the ch, back along its length.

Fasten off.

Thread the crochet ribbon through the loop and stitch the ribbon ends together.

It's definitely a winner!

Happy New Home

Mark that special move into a home of one's own – be it baby bungalow or penthouse apartment – with a cute, crocheted cottage. Just remember, there's no place like home...

Size

Height: 20cm

Materials

HOOK SIZE: 3mm

YARN:

Light brown for the walls and base

Blue for the roof

White for the windows and doors

Brown for the window frames

Red for the doorframe

Yellow and turquoise for the tiles

Emerald green for the grass

Dark green for the grass

OTHER MATERIALS:

Toy filling

Cardboard

Structure

Start by cutting cardboard to support the house structure.

The size can vary, however, edges that meet must be the same length.

The house shown:

Roof (x1), 10 x 14cm; fold in half so each half is 10 x 7cm

Walls (x1), 34 x 8 cm; fold into four sections of 10cm (front), 7cm (side), 10cm (back), 7cm (side), along the length. Join the end edges with tape.

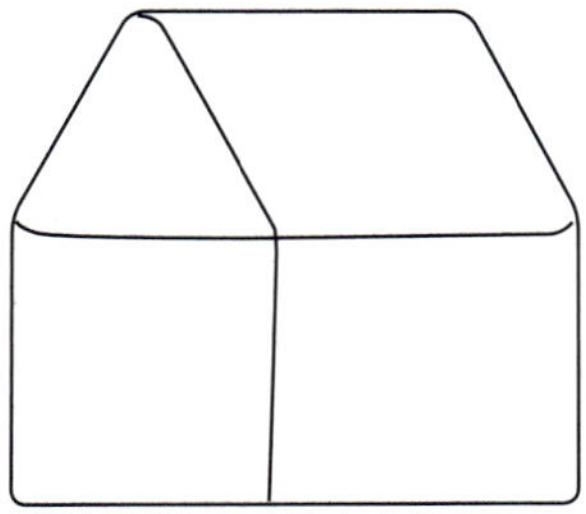

Front and Back (one of each)

Using light brown yarn, make a 21ch or a ch as wide as the section of cardboard for the front and back.

1st row: 1htr into the third ch from the hook, 1htr into each ch, turn.

2nd row: 2ch (counts as first htr), 1htr into the back loop of each dc, turn.

Repeat the last row until the piece measures 8cm or matches the depth of the section of cardboard for the front and back.

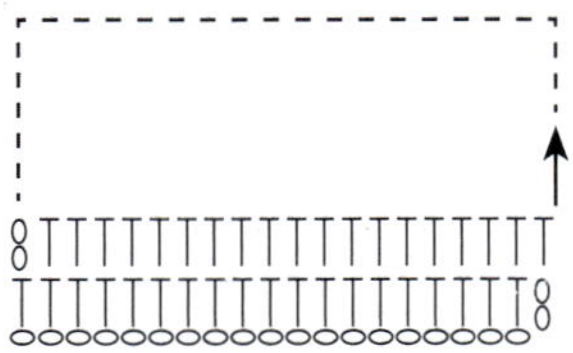

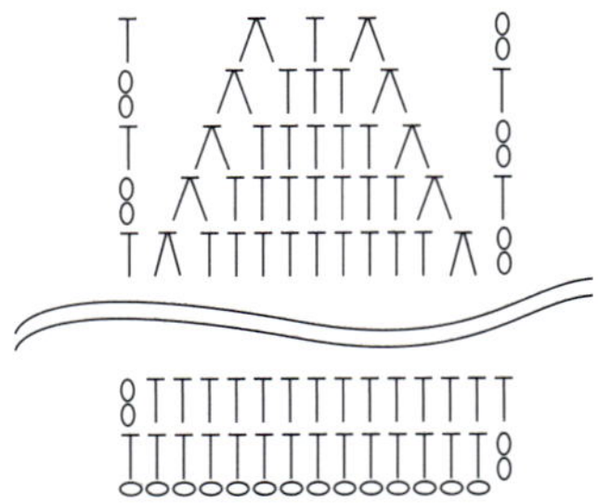

Sides (one of each)

Using light brown yarn, make a 16ch or a ch as wide as the section of cardboard for the sides.

1st row: 1htr into the third ch from the hook, 1htr into each ch, turn.

2nd row: 2ch (counts as first htr), 1htr into the back loop of each dc, turn.

Repeat the last row until the piece measures 8cm or matches the depth of the section of cardboard for the sides before the shaping.

Next row: 2ch, (counts as first htr), htr2tog, htr into each htr until 3sts rem, htr2tog, 1htr into last top of beg-ch, turn.

Repeat the last row until no sts remain and the selvedge measures 7cm or matches the depth of the section of cardboard for the roof – if necessary work decrease sts in the centre of the row.

Fasten off.

Base

Using light brown yarn, make a 16ch or a ch as wide as the section of cardboard for the sides.

1st row: 1htr into the third ch from the hook, 1htr into each ch, turn.

2nd row: 2ch (counts as first htr), 1htr into the back loop of each dc, turn.

Repeat the last row until the piece measures 10cm or matches the width of the section of cardboard for the front and back.

Roof (make 2)

Using blue yarn, make a 21ch or a ch as wide as the section of cardboard for the roof.

1st row: 1htr into the third ch from the hook, 1htr into each ch, turn.

2nd row: 2ch (counts as first htr), 1htr into the back loop of each dc, turn.

Repeat the last row until the piece measure 7cm or matches the depth of the section of cardboard for half the roof.

Fasten off.

Seam the two roof section together along the top edges of the last row.

Tiles

Using yellow yarn, join into the first line of exposed front loop of the roof section on the right edge.

1st row: [2ch, skip 1st, 5tr into the next front loop, 2ch, skip 1st, 1dc into next st] to end, ending with either a dc or 5tr sts.

Fasten off yellow yarn, and join in turquoise yarn into the next line of front loops.

2nd row: 2ch, 5tr into base of ch, 2ch, skip 1st, 1dc into next st, [2ch, skip 1st, 5tr into the next front loop, 2ch, skip 1st, 1dc into next st] repeat to end, ending with either a dc or 5tr sts.

Fasten off green yarn, join in orange yarn into the next line of front loops.

Repeat the last 2 rows until the desired number of front loops have been covered.

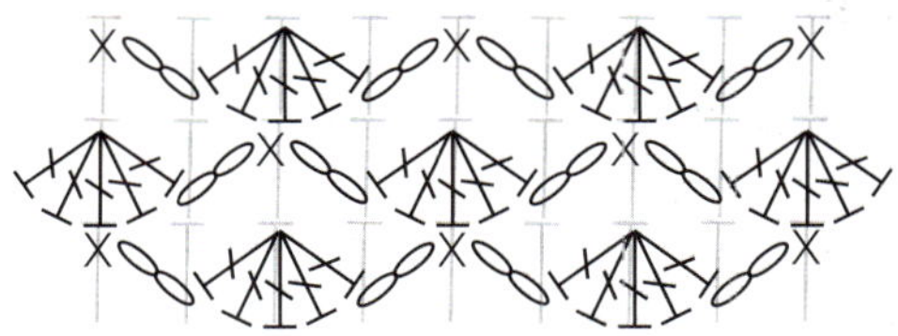

Larger grass section

Using emerald green yarn, make a magic ring as follows.

Make a loop with tail end of yarn on right, keeping ball end on left. Pull the ball end through loop. Make one chain through loop on hook you have drawn through to steady the circle. Work 6dc into the circle and complete with sl st into the first dc. See also page 13.

1st round: 2dc into each dc. (12sts)

2nd round: [1dc into next dc, 2dc into foll 1dc] 6 times. (18sts)

3rd round: [1dc into each of next 2dc, 2dc into foll 1dc] 6 times. (24sts)

4th round: [1dc into each of next 3dc, 2dc into foll dc] 6 times. (30sts)

5th round: [1dc into each of next 4dc, 2dc into foll dc] 6 times. (36sts)

6th round: [1dc into each of next 5dc, 2dc into foll dc] 6 times. (42sts)

7th round: [1dc into each of next 6dc, 2dc into foll dc] 6 times. (48sts)

8th round: [1dc into each of next 7dc, 2dc into foll dc] 6 times. (54sts)

9th round: [1dc into each of next 8dc, 2dc into foll dc] 6 times. (60sts)

Fasten off.

Smaller grass section

Using dark green yarn, make a magic ring as for the larger grass section.

Work as for the larger grass section until the 6th round has been completed.

Fasten off.

Front door

Using white yarn, make 7ch.

1st row: 1htr into the third ch from the hook, 1htr into each ch, turn. (6sts)

2nd–3rd rows: 2ch (counts as first htr), 1htr into the back loop of each dc, turn.

4th row: 2ch, skip 1htr, htr into the back loop of each of next 4dc.

Fasten off.

Using red yarn, join into the lower right edge and work a round of dc sts around the door.

Window

Using white yarn, make a magic ring as for larger grass section.

1st round: 2dc into each dc. (12sts)

2nd round: [1dc into next dc, 2dc into foll dc] 6 times. (18sts)

3rd round: [1dc into each of next 2dc, 2dc into foll dc] 6 times. (24sts)

4th round: [1dc into each of next 3dc, 2dc into foll dc] 6 times. (30sts)

Fasten off white yarn, join in brown.

5th round: [1dc into each of next 4dc, 2dc into foll dc] 6 times.

Fasten off.

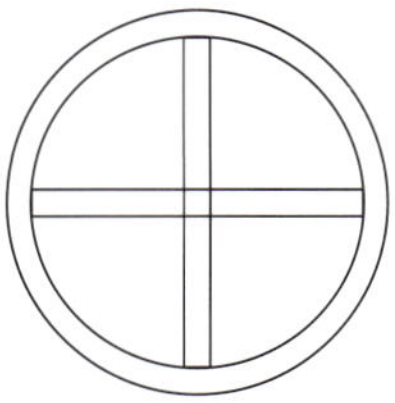

Making up

Using the structure diagram and photographs as reference, stitch the front, back, side and roof pieces. Place the cardboard inside the house against the sides and hold in place with toy filling. Stitch the base to the bottom of the house. Using red yarn and a French knot, embroider a doorknob onto the door. Using brown yarn and chain stitch, embroider window frames onto the door. Stitch the door and window in place. Stitch a short section of the two pieces of grass together. This is the house that you built!

Great Job!

Celebrate a step up the career ladder and crochet up this crazy little computer with its very own mousey mouse when you want to say congratulations on landing that plum new job.

Size

Computer height: 8.5cm

Mouse length: 5.5cm

Materials

HOOK SIZE: 3mm

YARN:

Grey for the screen and the mouse

White for the body

Yellow for the computer nose

Pink for the mouse nose

OTHER MATERIALS:

Toy filling

2 toy safety eyes, 8mm

2 black beads, 4mm

Structure

The computer is made up of a monitor and a base. The monitor is made up of three pieces, the screen, the back and one sidepiece, which is wrapped around four sides of the computer – all these pieces are worked in half treble stitches. And then there is a mouse, which is a mouse!

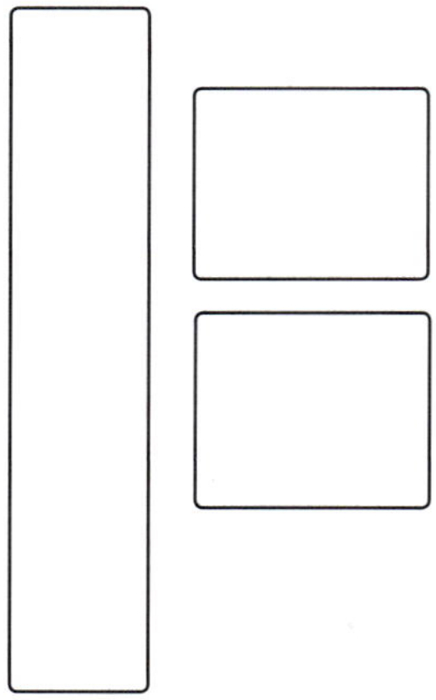

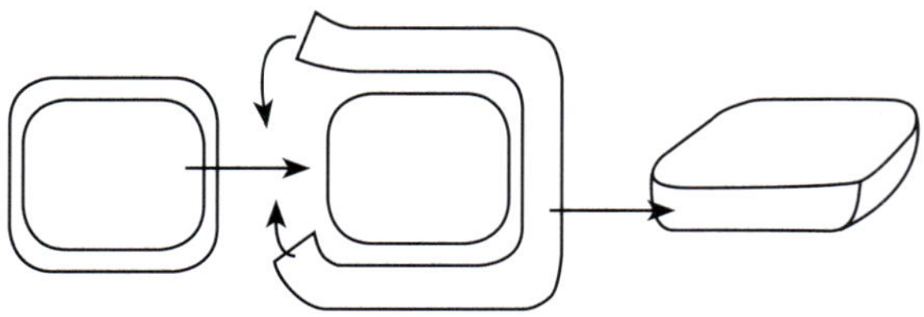

Computer screen

Using grey yarn, make 16ch.

1st row: 1htr into the third ch from the hook, 1htr into each ch, turn. (15sts)

2nd row: 2ch, (counts as first htr st), 1htr into each htr, turn.

Repeat the last row 4 times more.

Fasten off.

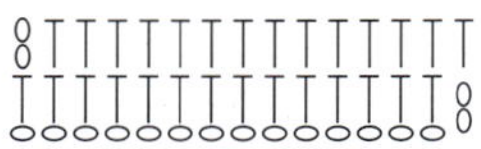

Computer back

Using white yarn, make 16ch.

Work as for computer screen.

Computer sides (make 2)

Using white yarn, make 6ch.

1st row: 1htr into the third ch from the hook, 1htr into each ch, turn. (5sts)

2nd row: 2ch, (counts as first htr st), 1htr into each htr, turn.

Repeat the last row until the piece will fit around the edge of the screen and computer back.

Fasten off. The two pieces need to be seamed and stuffed.

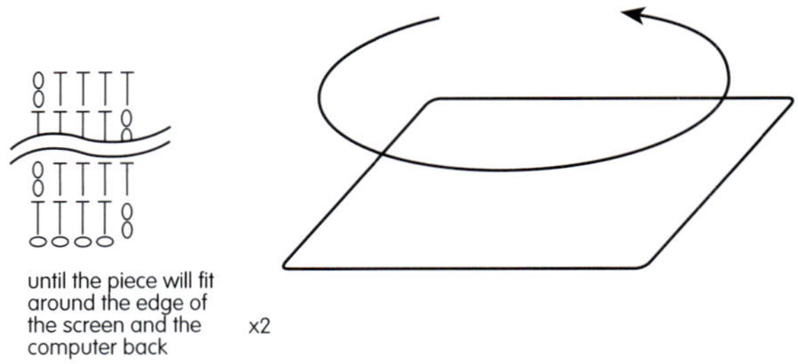

Computer base

Using white yarn, make 17ch.

1st row: 1dc into the second ch from the hook, 1dc into each ch, turn. (16sts)

2nd row: 1ch, 1dc into each dc, turn.

Repeat the last row 10 times more.

Fasten off.

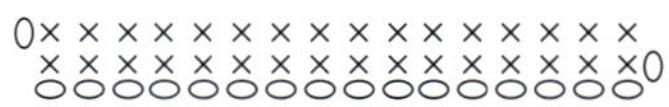

Computer nose

Using yellow yarn, make a magic ring as follows.

Make a loop with tail end of yarn on right, keeping ball end on left. Pull the ball end through loop. Make one chain through loop on hook you have drawn through to steady the circle. Work 6dc into the circle and complete with sl st into the first dc. See also page 13.

1st–2nd rounds: 1dc into each dc. (6sts)

Fasten off.

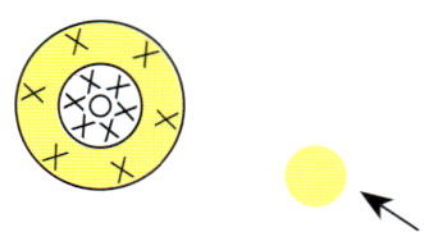

Mouse

Using grey yarn, make a magic ring as for the computer nose.

1st round: 2dc into each dc. (12sts)

2nd–3rd rounds: 1dc into each dc.

4th round: [1dc into next dc, 2dc into foll 1dc] 6 times. (18sts)

5th–9th rounds: 1dc into each dc.

Stuff the mouse with toy filling.

10th round: [1dc into next dc, dc2tog] 6 times. (12sts)

11th round: [dc2tog] 6 times. (6sts)

Fasten off.

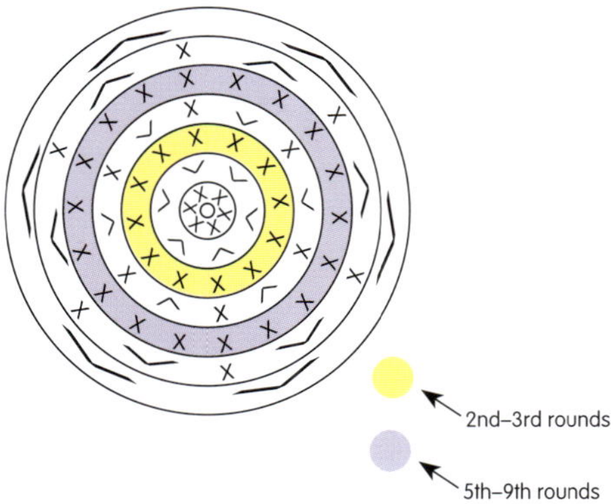

Mouse nose

Using pink yarn, make a magic ring as for the computer nose.

Fasten off.

Making up

Using the photographs as reference, attach the computer nose and toy safety eyes to the computer screen.

Pin the computer sides to the computer screen edge and using matching yarn, stitch in place.

Pin the computer back to the computer sides and sew the two pieces together around most of the outer edge. Fill with toy stuffing and complete the seam.

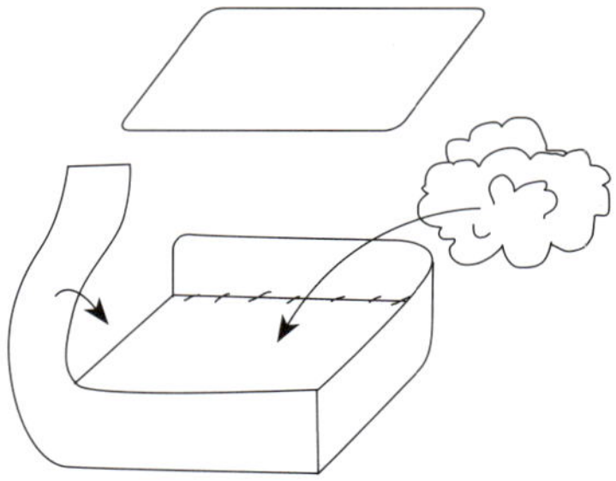

To finish the mouse: attach the mouse nose to the mouse; make ears by embroidering large loops on to the head; add whiskers by stitching through the nose, making a small anchoring stitch, cutting the yarn and leaving the ends free, repeat once more; stitch the black beads in place for eyes.

To connect your mouse to the computer, using grey yarn work a chain – there is no need for a USB cable!

Index

Resources

Enter the Happy Cute world of amigurumi. The following tried-and-tested retailers and suppliers can help you on your mission to fill your life with cuteness.

UK

Angel Yarns UK
www.angelyarns.com

Knitshop
www.knitshop.co.uk

Knit and Sew
www.knitandsew.co.uk

Laughing Hens
www.laughinghens.com

Loop Yarn Shop
www.loopknitting.com

Mason's Needlecraft
www.masonsneedlecraft.co.uk

Prick Your Finger
www.prickyourfinger.com

International

Blue Sky Alpacas, Inc
www.blueskyalpacas.com

Koigu Wool Designs
www.koigu.com

Patons
www.patonsyarns.com

Useful Information

If you are stuck for an idea or missing tools and materials, there is a serious online community support network of crochet and amigurumi enthusiasts. Check out The Knitting and Crochet Guild of the UK (www.knitting-and-crochet-guild.org.uk) and Crochet Australia (www.crochetaustralia.com.au) for crochet news, links to resources, and tips and advice. Try Etsy (www.etsy.com) for patterns, accessories, books, and all your other amigurumi needs.